Shopping for a Billionaire 3

by Julia Kent

I don't turn every date into a medical emergency, but when I do, I nearly castrate my man...

Shannon and Declan's first *real* date ends with an ambulance trip and yet another test of their madcap relationship. Ex-boyfriend Steve insists on dinner with Shannon while Declan is overseas on business, but a surprise return leads to plenty of romance as Declan whisks her away for a ride over Boston (in more ways than one...). Just as life and love look good, a misunderstanding takes on a sinister tone as a conspiracy brews to keep them apart. Julia Kent's hilarious *Shopping* series continues.

Part 3 of a 4-part series.

Sign up for my New Releases and Sales email list at my blog to get the latest scoop on new eBooks, freebies and more:

http://jkentauthor.blogspot.com/p/sign-up-for-my-new-releases-email-list.html

Table of Contents

Chapter One

The state park he chooses is really close to my apartment, but might as well be a world away. Large tracts of land dot the landscape as we tear down winding roads, bittersweet vines choking off large oak trees, the road dictated by old-growth trees as wide as cars. Omnipresent pines fill in the spaces between the oaks and maples, and the ground is covered with ivies ranging from the poisonous to the benign, invasively taking over much of the land.

An insect buzzes by and I jump. Not a bee. Whew.

Cracked trees still bear scars from the massive ice storm that hit this area nearly six years ago, the orange and beige colors dotting the view as we get out of the SUV and look around. The parking lot is small, bordered by large rocks that a few little kids are climbing on. A park sign and map aren't important to us, because Declan seems to know the way.

"How have I lived here for a year and not come here?" I wonder aloud. Three tree stumps sit side by side. The middle one is taller and has a rustic chess board hammered onto it, the outer stumps serving as stools.

"Maybe you need to take more risks and try new things," he says with a smile.

It's not quite dusk, so the sky still lights up the woods, but an ethereal quality infuses the air. Declan pops the trunk and it opens electronically, a slow ascent that seems too measured.

He pulls out a small backpack, a thick plaid blanket with waterproofing on one side, and another backpack, this one with a flat bottom. I grab my purse and sling it around my neck and under my arm, reaching for one of his cases.

"I've got them," he says.

"Let me carry something." He shrugs and I take the blanket. There is one wide path to the left, splitting the woods. It looks like an old road, but there is no sign of asphalt. The pale grey sky is a broad stripe above us on the walkway. The path curves up ahead, like a rolling strip of dirt ribbon.

"You come here often?" I ask as we start the walk.

"Now there's a pickup line."

I laugh, the air filling my lungs and making me chuckle far longer than I need to. I'm nervous. I should be. He reaches for my hand and his skin is warm and dry. He interlaces our fingers and we fit. Our bodies are aligned just so. We shift quietly into a walking pattern and he tips his head up to admire the sky.

"I don't think I need to find icebreakers with you," I say, turning to admire him. He looks back at me with a smile that lights my world.

His face goes serious, dimples gone, eyes

searching. "That's what I like about you, Shannon. I don't need to find anything when I'm with you. You just are. And being with you feels like living in real time. Moment by moment. Like I…" He dips his head down. Our shoulders are touching, and the strap from one of the backpacks slips a little.

The pause feels eternal.

"Go on," I say, giving him a gentle nudge. His hand in mine feels like a lifeline. Men don't talk about me this way. Men don't talk *to* me this way.

I want more.

He stops right in the middle of the trail and sets down the slipping backpack. His hand never leaves mine. Dusk is peeking through the clouds, the air a hair cooler than it was even a few minutes ago. The sound of the little kids playing at the parking lot fades, followed by the distant thumps of car doors closing. An engine starts.

Those green eyes look so genuine. Young and eager, nothing like the shut-off, shut-down man who argued with his father earlier this week, or who turned cold at our first business meeting the day we met. Declan opens himself up to me right here, right now, and I can't stop meeting his eyes. What I see in them is such a mirror of what I feel deep in my core that I go still with the possibility that everything I've tried to convince myself was impossible exists.

That makes Declan a dangerous man.

But I can't stop looking.

"Dating is so ridiculous," he says, his neck tight as he swallows. I can tell he's trying to hide his

3

emotions, and a part of me screams inside for him to keep the curtain pulled back. To call off the masons he's mustering to quickly rebuild that wall that separates him from the rest of the world.

The rest of the world includes me, and right now I want to be next to him, holding hands like this, hearts beating together and bodies relaxing with the relief of not having to be on guard.

"Yes." The less I say, the better.

He takes my other hand, and now we face each other, hands clasped. He's a head above me and I have no high heels, no oak-paneled walls, no dimly lit hallway as a refuge or a prop. We're a guy and a girl in the woods trying to figure each other out.

Trying to figure ourselves out.

"Women want to date me because I have money. Because I'm a McCormick. Because they can get something out of me, or gain some social or career advantage." His eyes flash and his voice goes bitter, but he never strays from my gaze. I will myself to maintain the look now, because I don't want to make him think I'm one of those women. I'm not. He could be a street musician who busks for a living and who has twenty-seven different recipes for ramen noodles and I'd fall for him like this.

That certainty slams into my heart like someone dropped a brick on it.

"But not you," he adds. "You had no idea who I was when we met." There's a lift in his voice at the end, not quite a question, but not quite a flat statement, either.

4

"No, I didn't. And it wouldn't have mattered."

He arches one eyebrow and takes a step closer. Our jeans rub together, thighs mingling. "Really?"

"I'm having more fun right now than I ever did Monday night," I reply, struggling to convey a feeling. It comes out wrong. When we just look at each other my intent is clearly communicated. Why do words have to make everything so complicated?

"Then I have to remedy that, because I can think of quite a few moments on Monday night that were way more fun than anything we've done so far." His grin has a lust-filled curl to it.

"I...Declan?" I have to say this. Have to.

"Yes?" He presses his forehead against mine. I look up.

"I don't want your money. I don't care about your money. In fact, I'm worried you're after mine."

He laughs.

And then I add: "But before we go any further, I do have something I want to ask."

"Go on."

"*Do* you have a toilet fetish?"

"Now you're just deflecting," he murmurs against my neck, then steals my mouth for a kiss that makes the world go light and dark, all at once, entirely through the connection of our bodies.

I break the kiss and look over his shoulder, back at the parking lot. "We've walked no more than a hundred yards."

"I guess we should actually hike on a hiking date." He picks up the backpack and we walk at a reasonable pace, our legs synchronized. For a few minutes silence is all we need. The crunch of old leaves on the path makes the air seem to have a soundtrack. Chirping birds and woodland creatures add to the sounds.

No one else is here.

"There's a clearing about half a mile ahead where we can set up," he explains. The path right now is straight but it goes up an incline, jagged rocks dotting the ground. I have to use a little effort to walk, and we let go of each other's hands to navigate.

I haven't felt this present, this in the moment, in…ever. With Steve there was always something to say, some mission to accomplish, some goal involved in whatever we did together. From going to the "right" movie to keep up on current trends to making sure we dined at a "fashionable" restaurant to be seen or to converse about the food at work parties, every minute we spent together had to be in service to some larger goal of helping him meet the next layer of life in the ladder of achievement.

Here I am, walking up a rugged path with a guy who is so many levels higher in business success than Steve, and all we're doing is walking among the trees to go sit and drink wine and eat strawberries under a meteor shower.

Wow.

And I wouldn't be anywhere else right now. Even my mind grasps that. It's leaving me alone, letting me soak in Declan and the sense of peace and greatness that comes from his attention.

We walk quietly until a small trail leads off. Darkness is hinting now, dusk making its entrance, and the newly sprouting leaves in the tall trees cast more of a shadow than they did even fifteen minutes ago. I'm guessing we're close to the trail. My legs don't hurt, but they're definitely noticing we've walked farther than the distance from my car to my office.

It feels great.

The trees clear quite rapidly until the full grey sky is open and brighter without the cover of tree limbs and buds. A wide stretch of matted weeds spreads out before us, clearly old farm land that hasn't been used for that purpose in decades. Because it's spring, the growth has a raggedy aspect to it, a mix of early yellow flowers, clover, and dead straw still hanging out from last year.

"Here," Declan declares. He stops just after we walk down a slight incline and reach a small spot of even ground. The optimal size for a big blanket. I'm tingling with anticipation and I take a second to remind myself to breathe. He's so gorgeous, and being out here in nature in a scene out of a National Geographic special (and not the kind on the mating habits of the albino rhinoceros) gives me a kind of thrill I can't quite describe.

Something fiery and settled, exciting and comforting. Distracted, I open the blanket and shake it out, gently spreading the perfect square on the grass.

A warm breeze hits us, belying the chilling air. "Make up your mind, New England," I say. "Is it winter or spring?"

He laughs. "And you say you've lived here your whole life? Remember the two feet of snow we got in '97? Or the inch that came in May back in 2002? Watch out. Mother Nature may be playing a trick on us with this balmy fifty-seven degrees."

"Every school kid remembers the April Fools' Day blizzard! That was awesome! No school for days!" My answer makes his smile deepen.

"You were what—eight?" he asks, bending down to sit on the blanket, digging in one of the backpacks to pull out a bottle of Chardonnay and a small white container of what I assume are the strawberries. My mouth waters. Not at the food. At the sight of his strong, muscled legs stretched out before him as he works a corkscrew on the bottle.

"Yep. That made you..." I do quick math. "Twelve?"

"Eleven. My birthday is in August. Sixth grade."

"Third for me."

I reach for the container and open it. Yep. Strawberries.

A loud *POP* announces the uncorking of the wine, and I rummage through the backpack to help find the wine glasses.

"Here," Declan says, reaching into the second pack.

He hands me coffee travel mugs.

"Huh?"

"Look closely." The tumblers are made of clear plastic with black tops, like coffee travel mugs. But when I look closely I see it—plastic pretend wine glasses built into the coffee mugs.

My laughter fills the night. "These are perfect!"

"Sippy cups for grownups. Grace highly recommends them."

"Then give Grace my thanks."

He unscrews the tops off the wine "glasses" and pours us each a healthy amount of white wine. Each movement is deliberate, careful, firmly in control. He puts the tops back on and hands me mine. We're sitting together, hips touching, knees up and braced. I'm comfortable like this. March was an unusually wet month and April wasn't much better for the first week. The ground is springy but not wet, the verdant greenery of the new plants poking out with sweet hope. A fly buzzes by my ear and I ignore it.

The view is gorgeous, as farmland and fields roll with glacier-made hills and valleys before us. A ring of thick woods surrounds the view, and it's a welcome relief from the chatter of the city just a few miles away. Route 9 is an endless string of mini-malls, regular malls, grocery stores, and chains, all buttressed by the city or Route 495 and its business belt. We're sandwiched between the suburbs, the city, and massive interstates, but in this quiet, reflective spot we could be anyone, anywhere, at any time.

I gulp the first half of my wine. A fruity flavor with just enough sweetness to make it easy to drink but dry enough to be enjoyable, I compliment him on the choice.

"Grace, again, I must admit," he confesses. No embarrassment. Just the gentlemanly acknowledgement.

"Then to Grace," I say, raising my tumbler for a toast.

"To Toilet Girl," he says with a playful smile.

Chapter Two

"To Hot Guy." We drink. We kiss. We sigh. He reaches for my now nearly empty tumbler and picks up a giant strawberry covered in dark chocolate.

"To first dates," he says as he hands it to me. My mouth fills with the second-best-tasting thing this evening, the first being him.

"This is our second date," I say around a mouth full of divine fruit and chocolate.

"It is?" He seems genuinely surprised. "I thought Monday was a business meeting."

He's playing me. I swallow quickly and grab my wine to finish it off and clear my mouth.

"If Monday was a 'business meeting,' I can only imagine how you define a 'merger,' Mr. McCormick."

"Is that a request for a demonstration, Ms. Jacoby?" His mouth is on mine before I can answer, tasting like fruit and happiness. His tongue parts my lips and this time he's more insistent, the earnest sweetness swept aside by a familiarity that grows between us. His hands envelop my waist and pull me to him as he reclines back on the blanket.

We're lying down now, his legs stretched out along my own, one knee pushing between my thighs as his heat seeks mine. He smells so good and tastes even better as his tongue runs along the edges of my teeth, hands in my hair, then down my back, caressing me like he owns me.

Or wants to.

My own hands can't get enough, and I shift, feeling his hardness against my belly. Knowing that he's hard for *me* sends an electric zing through my entire body, making me wet and needy. I've never felt such all-consuming want for someone else, a lust that threatens to wipe clean my common sense, to eradicate my inhibitions, to make me move and react from a place of primal desire.

His hand slides under the waistband of my jeans, hot skin against the small of my back, and I moan, that small sound of pleasure driving him to explore. His other hand slips over my breast, cupping it, and I take his touch as permission to see what I can discover on him.

This is a lovely game of I Spy. Except we're using our hands.

He fills his palms with my ass, his own throat letting a low growling sound that makes me wetter. The wind makes the field undulate as the sun peeks out from behind clouds, making a final, desperate attempt to shine before its day ends. All I can do is feel. My sex begins to throb, breasts swollen and plaintively wanting more of his body, his fingers, his touch.

His wanting me is the most erotic turn-on ever. Knowing he's hot for me, feeling his response to *my* presence, *my* mouth, *my* touch.

Me.

"Shannon," he whispers. Just my name. I understand, because his name zooms through my mind a million times a minute right now, trying to embed itself in deep grooves, to make it the only word I can think even when my mind is completely gone and I am nothing but sensation.

Declan.

This feels so good. So achingly good to have our hands and skin and lips and tongues all working together to get acquainted. He kisses my neck and one hand runs a long, luscious line up from my ass over my ribs to cup a breast from underneath, his thumb tweaking one nipple until it's rock hard.

I gasp. I want so much more. The movement pulls my shirt out completely from my waistband and I wiggle, primed for him. In addition to throwing EpiPens in my purse, I've added a handful of condoms because you really never know. Splendor in the grass…

"You are so lush," he whispers as he pulls away, my mouth raw and burning from so much kissing. I like it.

"You're amazing," I say as he pulls me on top of him, his erection pressing into my abs, my leg falling between his, thigh pinned between two powerhouses of muscled legs. I'm crushing him and he doesn't care, his caresses insistent and making it very clear that this could go as far as we want it to, all the way, and the Shannon that normally would demur is most definitely not the one in charge right now.

As he flips me over effortlessly, Declan's mouth crashes into mine with a roughness that I like more than I would imagine. He's covering me, the push of tight legs and his hardness on my inner thigh, his hand under my bra now, teasing and stroking until I'm throbbing. Nudging my legs apart, he continues to sweep my mouth with his tongue, leaving me breathless and intoxicated.

And not from the wine.

A fly buzzes near my ear and rushes off. Then a second. My shirt lifts up under his controlled hands and he works the clasp of my bra, freeing my breasts.

"You are so beautiful," he whispers as my shirt pulls up and he slides both hands over my swollen bosom, my breath catching in my throat, body completely vibrating for him.

Gently, he pulls me to the ground again until we're on our sides, hands exploring, mouths catching and releasing, my mind a blurred tornado of arousal. His hip nudges against mine and my hands go to his jeans, dipping down the front just enough to—

His groan gives me permission.

Apparently, my touch grants him a certain leeway as well, because his hands work the button of my jeans. Normally, I would pause. Date number two (or one? I'm not sure, and math isn't exactly on my mind right now) is a bit rushed for this, but I don't care. It feels right. It feels *so damn right*.

Freeing the front of our jeans simultaneously, we both go slowly, the curve of his lips on mine changing in its slope, our warm, wet exploration delicious and inviting, unwinding slowly as if we both recognize that time and space are ours.

His torso is like warm marble peppered with a sprinkling of hair, his hitched breath as I slide down that final half-inch deeply gratifying.

Cupid's arrow hits its mark just as he reaches my core and I gasp.

No—really. Cupid's arrow just stung my back.

"OW!" I shout, jolting up, my hand that just brushed against his thick rod now scrabbling across my rib. My bra is loose around my chest and a deep, intense burning is centered right on a specific spot on my back.

"What? What's wrong? Did I hurt you?"

I climb off Declan and sit on the ground, filled with pain and insta-worry that I've ruined the moment.

"No, no, not you." A freakish dread fills me as a fly buzzes in my ear again. And then one bites me on my back again.

That's not a fly.

"Oh my GOD!" I scream. "Get it away from me!"

Declan looks at me with alarm, his face drowsy with desire and the intimacy we'd just been in the thick of. His hands shoot to his waistband, where he quickly does his button and zips up.

"I didn't mean to push too hard or to ask you to do anything you didn't want to," he says in a rough voice. The look he gives me is confused and multilayered, open and closed at the same time.

I can't process is because my entire body is throbbing. Blood and adrenaline and venom pulse through me, a blind cloud of panic descending.

Then I kind of get it.

"Not THAT!" I shriek. "THAT can come near me any time!" I point in the general direction of his unzipped jeans. "I mean the bee!" Three lazy, floating bee bodies hover over us like unmanned drones centering in on a target.

"What?" he chokes out.

"Call 911!" I scramble for my purse, which is under the backpack. Throwing items randomly in the air, I realize time is precious. At best, I have a handful of minutes.

He frowns, then his entire face changes with dawning recognition. "You're *allergic*?" Something more than standard surprise fills his voice, but I can't parse it out right now, as my body begins to swell. His phone is out with breakneck speed and he's dialing before I can answer.

My vision starts to blur. Unadulterated terror sets in. The list of steps to contain the sting escapes me, all drowned out by the mental chant of OMIGOD OMIGOD OMIGOD that won't stop looping.

I lose track of time. Declan is speaking to someone and describing our location. Then he's off the phone and I find my purse. He fishes through his back pocket, pants loose around his upper thighs, and he takes a moment to pull them up, snap, zip.

Then his hands are on me and he's holding his

wallet. Two condoms poke out.

"Seriously? Now is NOT the time," I say. My voice is raspy and distant, like someone's scratching a cardboard tube shoved up against my ear.

"Not *that*—here." He hands me a foil packet of Benadryl, already torn open. I take the capsules and dry swallow them. I grab the tumbler of wine and, without any other option, I take a big swallow to make sure the pills go down.

"EpiPen?" he asks sharply. I recoil, even as my vision starts to pinprick.

"How do you know? And where did you get the Benadryl?"

"My brother Andrew is highly allergic, too. Wasps, in his case." He's tossing my tampons and old cough drops and receipts and makeup out of my purse with military precision and laser focus until he finds the EpiPen and hands it to me.

I pop the top off, but before I inject, another bee floats over. Looking down, I see the issue: we're near a nest of ground bees. The blanket is literally on top of them. Leave it to me to make out with Hot Guy on top of a Nest of Death.

Declan follows my gaze and realizes it, too. He reaches around me just as I tighten my grip on the pen and slam it as hard as I can into my hip, but he nudges me and my aim falters as I bring my forearm down as hard as I can so the needle goes deep in me to administer the epinephrine I need and—

I inject him in the groin.

"God DAMN!" he shouts, springing to his feet and inhaling so deeply I fear he'll pass out. One of us has to stay conscious, and at this rate it won't be me. A sound like rushing water fills my ears.

The Benadryl isn't helping, and that dose of epinephrine is the only thing keeping me from anaphylactic shock as I feel my breathing speed up, but my throat starts to narrow, as if Darth Vader has me in his grip and won't let go. Declan is limping and huffing, taking deep breaths and making grunting sounds as he comes toward me like Wolverine on the attack.

I fumble for my purse and keep trying to say "I'm sorry," but all that comes out is a strangled whooping noise. Declan grabs the purse from me and I can see the veins in his neck bulging, can watch his pulse throb in front of me as he pulls the cap off the second EpiPen, rolls me onto my stomach, pins me in place, and pulls my jeans down to expose my ass—

"What are you doing?" I rasp.

—and then slams the needle so hard into my butt cheek that the wind is knocked out of me.

The world goes dark, then light again as he scoops me up and begins running down the path toward the cars. He's favoring the hip near where I injected him, but still moves with remarkable speed and agility. My head feels so heavy, and my arms and legs flop, even though I know I should be surging from the EpiPen's contents. Maybe it's the wine. Maybe it's overwhelm. Maybe it's impending death.

"I'll get you there," Declan says. "C'mon, Shannon. Stay awake." That's an order, the hard grit in his voice like being barked at during basic military training, but his voice strains with fear and a gentleness that tells me I have to listen to him.

"I'm here," I mumble. He's running hard and I can hear his heart pounding against my ear, pressed against his sweaty shirt. We're more than half a mile from the parking lot and I hear a horrible wheezing sound. My weight isn't a small number, and I feel embarrassed that he's struggling so hard to breathe through carrying me. Yet he cradles me, mumbling something as he runs. All I can sense is the tumbling of air against his lungs and ribs.

If I could just move, I could stand and walk back to the lot. I start to resist, to try to help.

Then I realize the wheezing is coming from me. Not him.

He's moving swiftly and with great power, and my throat stops swelling. This is how the EpiPen always works, like slamming the brakes on a car going a hundred miles an hour. For me, the relief comes in waves. First, the swelling stops, but it doesn't recede. It just doesn't get worse.

That's what has happened now. I'm so tired, though. Exhausted and depleted, and it takes everything in me to stay upright in his arms so Declan can carry me. The ground becomes bumpy and he slows down, carefully navigating down a slope on the wider part of the trail. It's dark, and insects buzz in my ear.

"Bees?" I mumble.

"No," he says, his panting heavy from exertion. "Flies. But the two bees that stung you—"

He's huffing through a final sprint and I can make out a red flashing light in the distance.

Two. Oh. That's it. I've never been stung *twice* like this. My eyelids feel like quilts covering my vision, and my lips tingle and balloon out. If only I could lift an arm and give him some help. I will it to move but it doesn't. Nothing does.

I'm sorry, I want to say. Maybe I do. It's hard to tell.

And then I fade out completely, remembering nothing more than the steady sound of Declan's breath as he races me to safety.

Chapter Three

"Is his penis going to fall off?"

Mom's voice floats into my awareness as a big, bright light blinds me. Am I in heaven? Hell? Somewhere in between? If Mom's here, that narrows this down considerably. I'm either alive or in purgatory.

"Whose penis?" I mumble. "What did you do to Dad this time?" Someone squeezes my hand and I open my eyes slowly. They feel like wet wool blankets coated with glass shards, but I open them all the way anyhow.

Amy is the one holding my hand, and she looks so scared. "Not Dad. And don't worry."

My mouth tastes like dry pencil shavings that have been sitting in Death Valley for a thousand years. "Where am I?"

She names a local hospital.

"Why am I here?" My mind feels like dry pencil shavings, too. I'm cold suddenly, and my legs begin to shake. I have no control over this, and soon my chin chatters.

Mom grabs a stack of blankets and starts covering me in them, in layers up and down my body. The thick, heavy warmth cocoons me.

"You were stung by a bee, honey," Dad whispers, taking my other hand. I turn to look at him and his eyes are red-rimmed. Crying?

"Two, actually," Mom says.

"Daddy, don't cry," I mumble. "I'm sorry."

That makes Amy start to sob. "You don't have to apologize for something you can't control, Shannon," she says. "And thank goodness you're a paranoid freak," she adds.

"It comes in handy sometimes," I mutter, unsure what she means.

"You really scared us," Carol says. Carol! Carol's here, with a frightened-looking Jeffrey, who can't seem to look at me. Geez. Why is my seven-year-old nephew here? Haven't seen him in, what— a month? He's getting so big, with those long eyelashes and—has he been crying?

"Hi, Jeffrey," I croak out. He gives me an uncertain wave. I try to wave back, but a sharp stab of pain in my hand halts me.

An older female doctor with more salt than pepper in her hair strides into the room. It's not really a room, I see—there's just a curtain between me and another bed, where I hear two men talking in hushed voices.

The doctor looks at my chart and flips through pages, jotting notes. Her white jacket has little gold pins all over the lapel and she smells like freshly bathed dogs. Her face is tight. She looks up and realizes I'm awake.

"Shannon, that was close," she says in a clipped British accent. "I'm Dr. Porter." She sounds

22

like Judi Dench playing an older female doctor in a *Doctor Who* episode, because there are so many tubes and bright flashing lights in the room that I feel like I'm surrounded by Daleks that have taken over the TARDIS. "Good work by you and your date, though his aim was remarkably better than yours."

"Thank you," says a deep, familiar male voice from behind the curtain. "I agree one hundred percent. And Shannon, I'll never go target practicing with you. Ever."

Huh?

"And no, Marie, all my equipment is in place and intact. She got my *thigh*," the voice adds in a tone that makes it clear there is no follow-up discussion.

"Thank goodness!" Mom chirps. "Can't have grandbabies if it falls off," she whispers.

Maybe I'm the Dalek, because all I want to do now is scream EX-TER-MIN-ATE at her.

"I am five feet away and can hear every word," he growls. The curtain whips back in one smooth movement and there's Declan, alone, buttoning his jeans.

The memory floods me instantly. Wine. Hiking. Making out. Sex (almost...). Bees. EpiPen.

"I didn't break your penis, did I?" I rasp through vocal cords that feel like painful ribbons. Because that would be the Epic Fail of Dates. I would have to become a nun if I broke a man's penis. My name would become part of Urban Dictionary, like Lorena Bobbit. *"Why'd you stop dating Jill?" "Because she tried to Shannon Jacoby me." "No way, dude..."*

"What, exactly, were you doing out there?" the doctor asks, one eyebrow arched perfectly. She sounds so disapproving and snobbish, the way only a British person can, the accent so intelligent. "And no, you broke nothing. You're fortunate the denim on Declan's jeans helped to reduce the injury from the injection."

I try to hate her but don't really have the energy. Mom's words break through some of my angry confusion, but they leave me stunned and overwhelmed.

"No one broke anything, and I think everyone should go so I can take care of my daughter." She looks so defeated. Where's the sarcasm? The over-the-top exuberance and social cluelessness? The inappropriate oversharing?

Mom's eyes are swollen and hollow at the same time, and my throat closes again, except this time not from being stung.

I look at Declan, and he's looking back with so much concern that I close my eyes, unable to process anything.

"I was stung?" I murmur.

Mom scooches Amy over and takes my hand. Carol's holding Jeffrey's hand, with little Tyler perched on one hip, his eyes zeroed in on the television, which is set to Cartoon Network without sound. Jeffrey looks a lot calmer now, and he's watching Declan with narrowed eyes, like he's studying him.

Poor boy. His own dad never comes around, so maybe he's just checking out the Daddy crowd. Not that Declan's a daddy. Or is he? My head really hurts.

Amy and Declan share an inscrutable look. "Twice, honey." She slows her speech down, her eyes watching me carefully. All her makeup is gone and the hand that grabs mine is shaking.

They've all been crying. How bad was I?

"Did I die?"

Declan's face shifts to a quick expression of shock and he swallows, hard. He looks like he's about seventeen suddenly, wide-eyed and frozen.

Dad stands up and points to him. "No. But only because of him." Everyone turns and looks at Declan.

Steve would have smiled and taken all the credit if I'd been stung and he'd carried me out of there to an ambulance. As my brain starts to clear, I remember that Steve was there the previous time I was stung, back at UMass. That had happened on campus, and Steve had screamed like a little kid and run away, leaving me with my phone and my purse, digging furiously for the EpiPen.

He'd only come back after the paramedics arrived and I'd nearly passed out.

What Declan did was heroic in every sense of the word.

"We were half a mile—" I say. The rest of my sentence is choked off by my dry mouth.

Reading my mind, Declan grabs the pitcher of water on the tray above me and pours a glass that has a straw sticking in it. He hands it to Mom, who ministers it to me like I'm on my deathbed.

Am I?

"Early spring bees. Who knew they'd be out?" Dad says.

"That was my fault, sir," Declan says in a low voice. Contrite, even. "I chose the picnic spot and didn't think to clear the ground for bees' nests." He sounds angry. He should be. It was my fault for not telling him.

"Who would in April in Massachusetts?" the doctor snaps. I've never seen Declan like this, furious at himself, sheepish and so young looking, like he thinks he deserves to be upbraided for something that was completely out of his control.

"I should have." He looks at Mom and Dad. "My brother is highly allergic to wasps, and—" His face shuts down as he caps his emotions. My entire body aches, like someone is stabbing kitchen knives into my thighs, my butt, my neck and upper arms, but none of that pain compares to what my heart feels watching his reaction.

"No," I croak out. "You did everything right. You didn't know. I should have said something, but it's never been a big issue."

Mom snorts. "Shannon," she says in a chiding voice. Whether it's a "big issue" or not has been a bone of contention between us ever since I was first stung.

Then she squeezes my hand and looks between him and me. "You did everything perfectly, Declan." She lets go of my hand and stands,

26

grabbing him for an embrace. "You did everything perfectly, and thank you for saving my daughter's life."

My eyes start to water and two tears trickle down each side of my face, rolling into my ears. It itches. A tightness in my throat triggers panic in me. Too close to what I felt after the bee stings. My breathing becomes labored and the doctor checks my pulse.

"Slow breaths, Shannon," she says in a soothing tone. "The adrenaline is still in you and it will be a while before you're okay."

I nod, following her instructions. Mom's arm is thrown casually around Declan and they look like they've been best friends for years. It freaks me out and warms me at the same time.

Jeffrey clears his throat and opens his mouth. I see two white nubs along his gum line, the permanent teeth poking through. His nose is big and sunburnt and his cheeks have freckles on them.

"Yes?" I ask, giving him permission to speak in a crowd of scary grownups who tower over him.

It's Declan he turns to. "Did you break your penith?"

Oh, that lisp.

Suppressed snickers fill the room. We sound like a bunch of taste testers for canned baked beans after a new product line rollout. *Futt-futt-futt...*

"No, buddy, my penith—penis—is just fine." Declan reaches down and ruffles his hair. Jeffrey leans into the touch like a cat cozying up for some petting.

27

"Good." Jeffrey tugs on Declan's shirt. Declan bends down, but what comes out of Jeffrey's mouth can be heard by everyone.

"Jutht tho you know, you thouldn't play with your penith anywhere exthept in your bedroom. The penith is a private plathe."

Declan's eyes widen. Dad's hand flies to his mouth to cover a grin. Even the British doctor chick is trying not to laugh.

"Thanks," Declan says with a stage whisper. "I'll remember that *forever*."

Jeffrey's on fire now. A room of grownups paying attention, and a dad (in his mind, Declan's a dad, because all men over thirty are "dads") who is riveted by what he's saying.

"And you know what elth?" Jeffrey is king at court. He makes eye contact with every grownup as he takes roll.

"Yeah?" Declan is amused. He's confident and fine with a room full of adults making fun of his penith.

"You thouldn't let Auntie Thannon touch your penith. It's a private plathe and no one hath the right to touch it without your permithon. "

Oh, I had permission, bud. I can't, of course, say that, and the room is now filled with giggles and people biting their lips so hard they are causing de facto piercings.

Carol lunges for him. "Let's go get ice cream!" She mouths *I'm sorry* to Declan, who waves it off and gives Jeffrey a high-five as she scurries out the door with her boys.

28

Then Declan turns and faces the crowd. "You no longer have permithon to even *talk* about my penith."

"She needs her rest, anyhow, and I've had quite my fill of 'penith' jokes at this point," the doctor tells Mom and Dad. Declan lets go of Mom and shakes Dad's hand. My father pulls him into a manly hug and claps him twice on the back. It's a macho thing that would make me laugh if I had the energy.

Declan whispers something I can't hear to them while Amy kisses my cheek and squeezes my hand before letting go. "He ran with you the entire way to the car. The *entire* way." Her eyes rake over Declan's body in a way that makes me tingle with jealousy. Or maybe that's just my catheter shifting a little. Why do I have a catheter? How long have I been unconscious? "Even after you stabbed him in the crotch."

I snort. It hurts. Everything hurts. My eyes feel like slits in a slab of organ meat.

"How long have I been here?"

"About fifteen hours." She looks at her phone to check, and nods. "It's morning now."

"Jesus." I swallow. "Why does my throat hurt so much?"

"They had to put a tube down your throat to keep you breathing." She can barely say the words.

"Oh." I look at Declan, who is quietly talking to my mom. They keep looking at me with worried expressions.

"Not only do you manage to catch a

billionaire, you catch Captain America," Amy adds.

I try to laugh again but it comes out as a choke. She slowly lets go of my hand, trailing off, and follows Mom and Dad out as the doctor explains something to them about my care.

Declan and I are alone. And all I can do is start to cry. Big, messy tears that would devolve into a true ugly sobbing if I had the airway to spare. Instead, the fat teardrops just pour into my outer ear and collect there with a maddening itch.

"Why are you crying?" he asks with a tenderness in his voice that makes me cry even more. In seconds, he's across the room and stroking my hand.

"Because I almost destroyed your penith!"

The deep, booming laughter is so unexpected, like a sudden thunderclap on a clear moonlit night, that the sound shocks me and makes me choke out another apology.

He sits on the bed next to me and strokes my hair, tucking a long strand behind my wet ear. "Shannon, that was my fault. I moved and shoved your arm and you—"

"You're taking a lot of blame for what happened," I whisper.

He sighs, his neck and shoulders relaxing. "I do that when I think the woman I'm falling for is about to—" Declan swallows, his eyes boring into mine. Feeling his arm shake, his voice husky and low with worry, drains me of all my energy.

"It was that bad?"

"Let's just say I never, ever want to go through

that again."

"Good. Because you're allowed to have a toilet girl fetish, but not a bee sting fetish," I whisper.

The room goes still as he smiles with his eyes. No laugh, no chuckle. Then I realize what he's just said.

"Falling for me?" I ask.

Without answering, he climbs on the bed beside me.

"I, uh, I don't want to get pee on you."

"Isn't it a little early in our relationship for golden showers?"

I sputter, then gag, then cough for too long. I think I damn near fill the bag. "No, I mean…" I gesture to my pee bag.

"Oh. That." With a flick of his wrist he moves a tube just so. I'm on my side, so we spoon, and whatever he did makes it all work somehow. His hot thighs press against my backside, arm reaching over my waist and pulling me in. His touch is tender and careful, gentle and safe.

"Or do you have a hospital bed sex fetish?" I ask, yawning. I mean, really—hot, rich guy who saved my life and he's cuddling with me while I have a tube shoved up my urethra and I'm peeing in front of him? Only real in Fantasyland. Or Fetishland.

He lets out a low sound of amusement. "Believe me, of all the fetishes I could have, this is the last one on earth I'd want right now." I must have given him my yawn, because he joins in.

"You must be exhausted, too," I whisper. "I

pumped you full of epinephrine when I injected you. I'm so sorry."

He hugs me tighter. "It was an accident. And it's been, what—most of a day now."

How can he be so forgiving? Steve would have ranted for days about my injuring him, as if it had been a character flaw of mine. Declan takes my klutzy mistake in stride.

I pull away and half-turn to face him. "Accident or no accident, I put you in danger." I feel stupid and confused. The bed is small but his warmth feels so good.

"All I have to do is process out some extra adrenaline. My organs can take it. *You* came damn close to…" He won't say the word, so I do.

"Dying."

Tension fills his entire body from knees to hands. "Yes. Andrew came close when we were kids after a wasp sting. The whole family carries extra Benadryl at all times, and he has two EpiPens, too. It's not something you take lightly, and if I'd have known about your allergy, I never would have…" He sighs. "I would have made different decisions."

"That's my fault." My voice cracks. "I don't like to let it limit my life, and when you asked me for an outdoor date I didn't want to be—" I pause and yawn again. The room is getting dimmer and I hear the beeping from various machines down the hall. Machines that monitor heart rates and IV flow, that keep people safe and alive.

"What?" he asks gently.

"*That* girl. That weird girl who is sensitive and who lives a restricted life. Who imposes that on you." It occurs to me that maybe Steve didn't like picnics because of my bee allergy. That makes me frown. Perhaps he thought about me with more care than I realized. I seize inside, even though I do not have the energy for any of this.

Why am I thinking about Steve as Declan's scent fills me like the perfect prescription for healing?

"You wouldn't impose anything on me. I'm a grown man who can make his own choices." His voice is gruff. I don't feel vulnerable, though. This is an open give-and-take. I'm his equal. His very tired equal.

I yawn again. "Then I guess I was worried I'd give you one more reason not to choose me." I squeeze his hand and he squeezes right back.

"Why?"

"Because this is unreal."

He shifts against me, the rough denim of his jeans sliding against my bare legs. Sinking into the comfort of him, I sigh, a long, luxurious sound that feels like an endless exhale. As if I've been holding my breath for a year and can finally let it go. If you can't tell someone how you feel right after they've saved your life, when can you? Besides, if he doesn't return the feelings I can blame delirium for my confession.

"It is for me, too, Shannon," he says softly, his breath sending strands of hair against my cheek.

Oh! He's joining in. This is new territory.

He continues. "I can't believe that I found someone like you. And that you see something in me that makes you want to be with me." He swallows, and I can feel the movement on my shoulder. "I've spent years just chasing arm candy and bedmates." He's confessing to me, baring his soul.

I freeze, taken out of the comfort zone and into wishful-thinking territory.

"I'm not arm candy?" I try to sound lighthearted but instead I just feel raw.

"You're a chocolate-covered strawberry. A dozen of them. On top of a chocolate mousse cake." He nuzzles my neck, his smile imprinted under my ear.

"Do you really mean it?" I try not to sound as pathetic as I feel. Hope rises inside my chest, crawling out of a cave near my heart, shielding its face against the first shaft of sunlight it's seen in a long time.

He gets what I'm really saying. "Do *you*?"

"Do I feel the same way?" I break free from our spooning and very carefully turn over to face him. He's vulnerable and wanting, his eyes open and watching me carefully. No pretense. No shields. No walls.

"Yes." He's inventorying me.

"I can't believe you want to be with me. I'm... nobody."

"You're everybody," he says with a firm passion. His hand slides along my jaw and under the nape of my neck. "And watching you today, after

34

that bee...I can't lose you."

"You won't." I reach forward, the IV pulling on my arm, a sharp, needling pain making me wince. He pulls the tangled tube away from its knot with such care I want to cry from the joy of being treated like this.

"How about we both just stop right here."

My heart seizes. "What do you mean?"

"This is what we both feel. It's real. It's *real*," he says with urgency. His lips press against mine and the kiss is so sweet that tears spring to my eyes. His body moves toward me and stops. He pulls back and closes his eyes. "And it's so real that we need to let down our walls and let reality guide whatever comes next."

"I have always lived in Realityland. I'm the mayor of it. It's the rest of the world that doesn't cooperate."

He smiles.

"No, seriously. Have you met my mother?"

Now he just shakes his head with amusement. We both yawn at the same time, slow, lion-like sounds. I turn back around and he snuggles up.

"Are you allowed to nap with me?" I ask. I think half the words disappear as I fade off to sleep.

"It's better to ask forgiveness than permission," he says, the vibration of his words against my neck a cozy feeling. A feeling I could get used to experiencing every day of my life. "Besides, the nurses take pity on me. They're also a little jealous of you."

"Jealous?"

"When I had to strip down to show them the EpiPen puncture, they got an eyeful."

My laughter is quieter than I want it to be. I'm so tired.

"Is this the weirdest date you've ever been on?" I mumble as sleep overtakes me.

"Probably." A long pause, and then he adds, "The EpiPen was definitely the most inventive sex toy a woman has ever used with me."

I'm in a state of exhausted bliss, and as I float off, a thought occurs to me.

"Declan?"

"Mmm?" He's breathing slowly, his voice muted in the tiny room. I almost feel bad interrupting him, but I have to know. The thought won't go away.

"How did your mother die?"

His breathing halts, the warm muscles behind me solid and tense like granite. Then he relaxes, as if by will. The monitors ping on.

"It's not important. Go to sleep, honey."

"You called me 'honey,'" I whisper, my eyes filling with tears. He can't see me, and that's good.

"I'm just so, so grateful you're going to be okay." His hand rests on my hip with a possession and a familiarity I like. I like it very much, but I'm so, so tired.

"Thanks to you," I mumble, and then that's all there is.

Chapter Four

The first date I have after I get out of the hospital feels like a combination of a bad *Girls* episode and sealing myself to the bathtub during an unfortunate do-it-yourself waxing session.

What? Why do you think my mother insists on making me go with her to the spa? She let me get out of it this week because of billionaires and bees and that whole Shannon-almost-died thing, but I know it's coming soon.

This bad date, though—it turns out it's going to be a doozy. The kind of night where you go on Truu Confessions and skewer the person, then it becomes a BuzzFeed article and the next thing you know you have a podcast that propels you to a cable show and then—

"I wish I had been there, Shannon," Steve says in a low murmur. That's right. I'm on a date with *Steve.*

Not Declan.

Declan is off in New Zealand slaying Orcs or whatever you do "on business" in New Zealand. He almost offered to bring me, but the whole IV-in-the-arm thing and my mom's screams about New Zealand bees killing her daughter put a stop to that.

"Bad timing" will be etched on my gravestone, I swear.

Plus I have a backlog of shops to do, including two podiatrist offices (checking fungal safety protocols), one cigar shop (to see if there's clerk bias against women), one massage company (hallelujah!), and fourteen fast food restaurants testing out a new Caesar salad.

Fortunately, I like anchovies. Amanda's allergic to them (she says...), so I know what I'll be eating for lunch for the next three weeks.

Last night I got into a lovely sexting session with Declan that ended in some pictures of him and a few pictures of me and let's just say thank God for the fact that pictures you take on Snapchat all get deleted within a few minutes, because if this relationship goes south there would be pictures of me in compromising positions way more embarrassing than a hand in the toilet.

Steve is, instead, my "date." He keeps calling it a date, and I keep calling it, well, *nothing*. We're at a local Mexican joint where all the food is homemade and delicious, but coated with cilantro the way my mother puts on mascara. Three layers deep and with a ruthless efficiency few can master. At least none of the cooks poked my eye out while applying it.

"If you'd been there it would have been awkward, Steve," I say in a no-nonsense voice, though I reach forward and pat his hand. That's such a patented Marie Jacoby gesture that I freeze and snatch my fingers away as if I'd been burned.

They say you turn into your mother as you age. Kill me now.

Weird. It's so weird to realize how much of your parents seeps into you unconsciously. Pretty soon I, too, will wear nothing but yoga pants and use push powder to fluff up my thinning hair while talking incessantly about Farmington Country Club weddings and my dildo collection.

And if I had married Steve, that pretty much would have summed up the next three decades. I shudder again and shove a fried tortilla chip in my mouth to stifle a groan.

"Why would it have been awkward?" he asks, one corner of his mouth turned up in what I assume is an attempt to give me a seductive smile. He looks like the Joker, minus makeup.

I chew fast and swallow hard. "Because Declan and I were on a date." Do I really need to spell out the obvious?

"Got a problem with two men at once?" he says in a guttural tone I've never heard from him.

"What the hell is wrong with you?" I bark. "And ewwww, who wants two men at the same time?" One is hard enough to handle. If I want two men at the same time then one of them can change my oil while I have sex with the other one. Now there's a fantasy.

Steve just laughs and says, "I thought you two weren't dating." He uses both hands to pick up his drink, which is a strawberry margarita the size of a bucket. You could host a pool party for toddlers in there.

I cock one eyebrow and try not to sigh. "You caught us kissing at the restaurant two weeks ago. We're *dating*." My voice is firm and kind of flat, the way you talk to a pollster during a presidential campaign. Like you want to be nice and do your duty, but c'mon—let's get this over with so you can go off and spin this conversation to your advantage in the most sociopathic way ever.

"That doesn't mean you're dating." He takes three enormous swallows of his drink and sets it down, salt coating his thin upper lip. Steve then unrolls the silverware from the yellow cloth napkin and shakes the cloth onto his lap. His hands are steady but something is off. Why am I here again?

Whatever ambiguity I felt when Declan and I dined with Steve and Jessica is gone. Long gone, and now replaced by apathy. Something even less than apathy, though. A growing annoyance that makes me see Steve is part of my past. Not my future.

The clarity makes me ache for Declan right now. Of all the times to be in New Zealand, frolicking with Hobbits. Hobbits have nasty feet. My mind drifts to the podiatrist visits I have to complete later this week.

"I don't routinely shove my tongue down the throat of people I'm not dating." The words slip out before I even deliberate whether to say them. If Amanda were here she'd be cheering. A few weeks ago I'd have never challenged Steve like this, but a few weeks can change *everything*.

He pauses in mid-movement, nostrils flaring,

then he's the one who sighs. "I'm not sure I know that for a fact, Shannon." His eyes snap up and catch mine. The look he gives me is hard and accusatory.

"What is that supposed to mean?"

"I think you're dating him to make me jealous."

Thunk. That's the sound of my jaw falling through the earth's crust, magma, core, and splashing into Declan's lap in New Zealand.

"You think I'm—"

"It's brilliant!" He takes a long draw off his drink. "Seriously. Making sure you pick the same restaurant where I'm with Jessica. Using Jessica's online presence to help boost your profile—"

"What?" Where does he get that from? I want to be tweeted about by Jessica Coffin about as much as I want to suck on Steve's toes. "You think I'm jealous of you and Jessica and I'm dating Declan McCormick to…to…what?"

"Get me back."

A deeply wheezy sound emerges from my throat as the tortilla chip I shoved in there lodges itself in the worst way possible. I'm not in danger of choking to death. Just gagging in pain until the offending object moves out of the way.

Hmmm. That kind of describes Steve, actually.

The tortilla chip cracks and goes down (and no, that doesn't describe *me*), and with a big swig of my water glass I finally look at him with tears in my eyes from having my throat lacerated by a completely innocent piece of food.

"You think I want you back?"

He takes a big chip, dips it in the salsa, bites off half, and double dips. That's right. He just offended Jerry Seinfeld and the crew with one bite.

"Of course you do. it's been a year, you're still single, and you're here. With me. On a date. So—it worked." He spreads his hands magnanimously, as if accepting defeat for some battle I didn't know existed. "You win."

"I win *what*?"

"You win *me*."

"I don't want to win you! I never win anything! If I'm going to win something, it should be an all-expenses paid trip to Puerto Vallarta or a Kia Optima, not an all-access pass to be the slobbering, under-appreciated girlfriend to an over-important fleshbag who thinks I'm inadequate and who has an ego bigger than his penith!"

Well, now. Who knew that was in me? He doesn't seem offended, though. More worried that other people heard me, but not actually upset by the content and meaning of my words.

"You're not the woman I thought I knew."

"You mean the woman you *rejected*." I reach for my own bucket of sugar and alcohol and take a few gulps of liquid courage. Mine is a cranberry margarita, which sounded way better when I read it on the menu. It tastes like a cough drop mixed with Love's Baby Soft perfume.

"'Rejected' is such a harsh word." Steve splays his massive hands across the table and stretches forward, as if he wants me to hold hands. Nope.

"No kidding it is. It *hurts*."

Our eyes lock and I realize that just like I don't understand why I'm here, *he* has no idea why he is here. For the past week since I got out of the hospital he's hounded me to get together, and now he's got me. All my attention, all my focus. But he has no idea what to do with me.

"And that's why you don't reject a woman like Shannon. Ever."

The growling voice comes from behind me and I literally jump in my seat about three inches, falling back down onto the hard wood with a jolt that spreads up from my tailbone and through my eyeballs. Which are currently locked on Steve's shocked face.

He is staring at a point behind me, above my head.

I whip around, knowing that voice, and my breath catches in my throat. Declan's standing there, a day's worth of stubble peppering that strong chin, his business shirt unbuttoned at the top, no tie, and he's delightfully rumpled, his grey suit wrinkled in all the right places, pants tight and tailored to fit like a glove. He looks like he just spent the entire day in motion, and as my eyes take him in he looks at me greedily.

His hand slides along the bones of my shoulder, cupping the soft skin at the back of my neck, and his lips find mine for a gentle, polite kiss that makes me throb everywhere. Sexting last night wasn't enough. Never enough. I swallow hard as he pulls back, the scent of him full of sweat and cologne and soap and *home*.

"Hi," he says to me, eyes claiming mine. Steve clears his throat. *Steve who?*

"Good to see you, Declan." Steve stands and offers his hand. Declan completely ignores him, his eyes boring into mine, hand on my neck like he's drowning and touching me is the only way to breathe.

"Hey," Declan finally says in Steve's general direction.

"We were just talking about—" Steve starts to say, but Declan interrupts him.

"How you rejected Shannon." Declan's words are granite. Iron. Platinum. Take the hardest element and multiply it by every time Steve told me I wasn't good enough and you come close to Declan's voice.

I feel like I'm in a bubble. My skin is tingling and burning with exposure. People don't talk to each other like this in my world. We aren't direct and clear with our boundaries like this. We don't make declarations like Declan, firm "no" statements that Steve is flat out wrong for trying to shame me —rather than *me* being wrong for whatever he's trying to shame me over.

That invalidation is the greatest sin.

I've been taught to joke my way through discomfort. To let people cross my internal lines because that's fine—they love me, and besides, maybe it's okay. No big deal. *Ha ha*, laugh off that feeling in the pit of your stomach that says this is wrong. *Hee hee*, go along with the joke at your expense because pointing out the truth will make

44

everyone *else* uncomfortable.

With Steve, I kept thinking all those years that if I could "just" change enough to stop his newest criticism, then I'd be perfect. If I could "just" be on edge all the time and try to guess what my next misstep would be in his eyes and stop myself before I transgressed, then he would be happy with me.

If I could "just" learn to live life according to mixed signals and constantly shifting expectations …which meant I would never, ever be good enough.

Ever.

A jumble inside me feels like shattered glass being moved and realigned with great care, like reassembling a broken mosaic to put it back in place with the least damage possible. Declan has armor I cannot imagine wearing. He has a core that knows who he is and what he wants without the reflection of others. No mirrors pointed back at him telling him to internalize what everyone else thinks of him.

If I hadn't touched him, kissed him, joked and teased and played with him, I would think he was a god. But no…he's flesh and bone and real and authentic and…

Mine.

And I am enough for him. Enough as is.

More than enough.

And that is true even without Declan.

"I—" Steve is speechless. Declan's godlike status just went up a notch, because Steve's bloviating is hard to stop, like trying to stop Mom from getting up at 2:30 a.m. on Black Friday to stand in line at a big-box store and come home with a television bigger than the height of our house because "It was only $39.97! and they gave me a free coffee!"

"Come here," Declan says, pulling on my hand. He's crossed oceans for me. Cut meetings short. Slept in airplane seats designed for children who aren't tall enough to ride rollercoasters. His pull leaves no question, no opportunity to argue. I'm going with him, and Steve's nostrils flare.

"What are you doing?" Steve asks. He doesn't ask, though—the words come out in a livid monotone. Years of dating and he'd never shown jealousy toward any other guy, even when we'd been at nightclubs and someone grabbed my ass. No protectiveness, no possessiveness, no sense that he was upset that I was someone else's hand candy, objectified and easy for a grab that meant nothing and everything at the same time.

All those years of being his...*what*? What was I to him?

"I'm taking Shannon," Declan says in a tone that is the mirror opposite of Steve's—full of passion and infused with feeling. His words are measured but the meaning behind them isn't.

She's mine. You fucked up. Go away.

Wait. Those were the meanings behind *my* words, actually.

Declan pulls a wallet out of his back pocket, his other hand firmly holding my elbow with a grip that is not unpleasant. He tosses two twenties on the table and with a gentle nudge turns me away from

Steve, who sits there, impotent, staring gape-mouthed at the cash.

Declan's steps eat the floor between where I'd been sitting and the main door, my legs like tingling rubber bands as I work to match him. The way he just treated Steve makes my brain buzz. It was so... rude. So...macho.

So...*right*.

Chapter Five

"Thank you," I say as he pushes the door open and a burst of sunset explodes before my eyes, feeling returning to my legs, my lips, my body. As the steps take me away from a man who had never cherished me, never seen me as anything more than a tool, I feel my body fill in.

Like a paint-by-numbers project, here comes my dignity in a lovely shade of purple. Blue stands for confidence. Rich red for clarity. A sedate adobe represents patience, and green is the color of hope.

Declan's eyes.

"For what?" he asks as he holds the car door open for the (of course) waiting limo outside the restaurant.

"For that." I thumb toward the restaurant, half expecting to see Steve's distorted face pressed against the plate-glass window. "Um, how much did you hear?"

"You mean the part about his tiny penith and his huge ego? Because that was great." A half-grin and hearty laugh follow. "'Penith' will never not be funny."

Declan's hand is on the limo handle when I realize—my car!

"Wait. I drove here," I explain, a sinking feeling hitting me at once. Practical Shannon. How would I get home if Price Charming sweeps me away on his mechanical steed?

"Turdmobile?" he asks. A passerby gives him a funny look, staring at the limo with one eyebrow cocked.

"Yep." I look over at the parking lot where I stashed the damn thing. Even mixed in with a bunch of late-'90s junkers, the car stands out like my mom at a Submissive Wives conference.

"I'll bring you back," he says, opening the door. Declan slides in next to me, shutting the door with a sound that sends a thrill through me. We are hermetically sealed in the cool leather, the divider firmly up so that all we are is a man, a woman, and a bunch of alcohol in the back of a car bigger than most dorm rooms.

"Thank you again."

"That was nothing."

"That was *everything*."

The ferocious, feral nature of the kiss he gives me before I can finish saying the final word tears away at any restraint I pretend to have. As his mouth devours mine, his hand slides up under the thin cotton skirt I'm wearing.

"Mmmm, skirt," he says against my lips. Apparently my flesh has the ability to make him lose entire grades of vocabulary. Who knew? His fingers take advantage and slide right up my quivering thigh. He's not teasing.

He's very, very serious.

Today is not supposed to be the day. *That day* is supposed to be carefully planned, with roses and good food and wine and a carefully manicured Shannon. *That day* should involve a giant full-body waxing session, a few pokes in the eye with Mom's mascara wand, and a trip to a lingerie shop filled with self-loathing and best-friend reassurance that spending $200 on pieces of silk Declan will tear off my body in seconds is totally worth it.

Right now? Here? I have leg stubble that is coarser than snapped pine trees after an ice storm. My lady place hasn't been trimmed in so long it looks like Malcolm Gladwell's hair. Small woodland creatures probably make their home in there, and while I did (thank God) shower this morning, it's not like I thought my cobwebs would need to be cleaned out today.

Of all days.

He's breathing slowly against me, body curled up and over mine, hovering and so…male. Being wanted like this by a man who is the undisputed leader in any given room full of penises is a turn-on, and my mind shuts off as the body takes over, his fingers making that all too easy as he finds my throbbing center.

Oh, he really is a god after all.

The way he strokes me, slow and deliberate, as his tongue works in concert with his fingers, my mouth and sex both wet and wild, brings me to the edge so fast. I'm so ready.

I want him so much.

The car pulls away from the curb and I giggle

as we lurch, his erection pressing into my hip. His face is dark with want. I'm wet with need. We're a match made in limo.

I undo his pants and reach in to grip him, the sharp hiss of air sucked in through his teeth my reward. I pull his pants down enough to look and see what I never got a chance to gaze at before we were so rudely interrupted by the Bee Who Nearly Killed Shannon.

He's beautiful. Thick and veiny and big, skin soft and vulnerable.

"I didn't break your penis after all," I say. I can see a tiny puncture mark with a fading bruise, though, just an inch or so away from the base of him. If I'd been just slightly off…

"No, you didn't. But maybe you will tonight. In the best of ways." His hands roam over my back, skimming the surface of my skin, then pressing with more urgency.

I laugh, a sound of anticipation.

"Are you evaluating me? Am I aesthetically pleasing?" he asks in a throaty chuckle. "Do you have your app ready to write up your review?"

My answer is to release him and push him back against the seat. I throw one leg over his lap and straddle him, settling over his unleashed self, the thin cotton triangle of my panties the only thing keeping us apart.

"You're part of a new project. The Shopping for a Billionaire Project." I wiggle just enough to make him groan.

His hands slide under my shirt, cupping my

breasts, and with a grace that makes me moan he unclasps my bra and wraps those big, strong palms around my breasts.

"How am I doing so far?"

I make a noise of contemplation. "Eh. Six out of ten."

He arches one eyebrow, clearly displeased. "Six? I don't *do* six."

I wiggle against him, the shaft sliding along my nub, making my next words come out with a quaking tone. "No, you're no six." I close one eye and slide up, shivering. "Maybe seven?"

His abs tighten, shaft lifting just enough to make little light bursts appear, somehow making an entrance in my open-eyed vision.

"Six? Let's go for ten," he insists. The snap of my panties registers for a second as a sharp, cutting pain against one hip as he rips them off me. All that separates us now is something deeper than decency.

Declan senses it, too, and shifts just enough, reaching into his back pocket for his wallet. The condom appears and he puts it on as I watch his hands, his face, marveling at the unreality of the moment.

Yet it feels more real than anything I can fathom.

He guides me back into his lap and I settle my thighs around his hips, his tip at my entrance like a beacon, mutual throbbing making a pulse that joins two rhythms.

And then he's in me, kissing my neck, pulling my shirt up over my head, bra hanging from a door handle and he thrusts up into me, thumbs on my nipples, my body burning for more.

More more more.

The thrill of his fullness in me, of the movements as he kisses me, slow, languid kisses so lush and patient. The kind of kiss you give someone when you mean it. When you want to be with them.

When they're enough.

More than enough.

"I have wanted you since the first time we met," he says, serious and breathing hard, his hands on either side of my face, eyes lasered in on mine. A shock of hair falls over his forehead and the day's beard gives him a rakish look, even as he's tender and loving.

"You rivet me, Shannon. You make me want you more than I want to be in control, and no woman has ever done that. I abandoned a merger negotiation in New Zealand because I kept looking at our text stream and wondering why the fuck I was settling for pictures of you when I could be inside you."

Oh!

I don't have any words. He hammers his point home and I gasp, tightening.

He groans, breaking our gaze, pulling me in for a kiss that tastes like promises and desire.

"I needed you. Need you. Need this," he says, pulling his hips back, clenching his abs, then sliding back up, making me pitch my head back, the sensation too immense to take in just through one part of me. My arms, my face, my flushed skin, it

54

all feels like it's part of Declan, and he's part of me, and we're both part of the sky, the clouds, part of everything.

"I need you, too, Declan," I say as I tip my head back down and unbutton his shirt. The feel of his hot skin as I skim my palms across his pecs makes me wetter, the heat from our coupling like my own star, bright and radiant. "I can't quite believe this is happening. That you're with me. That we're here."

"You're hot and warm and tight," he groans. I pull in, making my core strong, and he makes a primal sound that is both threatening and satisfying. I made him do that. *Me*. His thumbs caress my hips and I surge for a second, shivering with a quick tingle. A moment of self-consciousness kicks in as his hand caresses my belly under my skirt, thumb pad stroking down again to find the spot I want him to touch the most.

But the palm across my belly makes me think about my curves. My abundant flesh. My...extra. My *too much*.

He frowns, watching my face. "What's wrong?"

"Nothing." The word comes out breathy and forced, like a cheerleader whose leg fell off but she's in denial, still completing her program. *Damn it. Don't do this, Shannon. Don't ruin it.* You would think I'd have felt this way when we were at the park, or the first time we kissed, or the times he's touched me intimately, and yet – no. It takes being in a limo, surrounded by the trappings of wealth and status for me to feel this sense of inadequacy, quite suddenly.

I know exactly why, and it sucks.

The first time Steve ever hinted that I might not be good enough was, of course, in a limo. My junior year in college and we were on our way to some business networking event. He'd evaluated me from top to bottom and found the cut of my dress "a bit outdated" and asked whether I'd been exercising enough lately.

I ate a small salad for dinner that night.

Declan cocks his head and stares me down, thumb stroking until I move involuntarily, the self-consciousness replaced by a growing wave inside.

"Tell me," he murmurs.

"No—really." The slow circles he traces in my most private flesh are like a language he's transmitting through these maddening finger presses.

"Tell me," he says again in a voice that makes it clear I can't escape.

"It's...my body." As sunset descends, the shadows outside pass by like a crowd in motion, except we're the ones moving. The limo glides left, then right, and Declan and I float with it, micro-movements sending waves of grinding want through me as the pressure of his fullness in me touches little fragmented spots that send my body thrills I didn't know I could feel.

"Your body is..." His voice drifts away as his eyes rake over me, methodical and appreciative. I'm not used to this. Sex is frantic groping in the dark, where I'm glad for the cover of the obscurity of darkness. What Steve or other lovers felt when they touched my skin was so much easier to handle than imagining them look at me. When they touched me under covers or in the grey night, I could just feel and enjoy.

I'm watching Declan look at me and feel my self-consciousness melt away, like a layer of skin that sheds gently. His eyes are hooded, filled with craving, and as his gaze lands on my breasts I can almost feel him, his eyes like fingertips searching for truth and love.

"Your body is beautiful," he says gruffly, as if contradicting someone who said otherwise. And, actually, he is. All the voices who tell me I'm imperfect. The moments when Steve looked at rail-thin women in public, or the *harumph* of telling a store clerk I needed a size sixteen.

The internalized, yappy-dog chatterer that has taken up residence behind my ear and that lets loose a steady stream of thoughts and feelings about my loose skin on my belly, the lush breasts that never fit quite right in my bra cups, the pants that don't smooth neatly across my waistband, the thick, muscular calves that rub against the finely tailored wool of his pants.

That voice.

"Beautiful," he says with a tender thrust upward, pulling me down for a kiss. His tongue slides between my lips and he's telling me again how beautiful I am, except this time with the topography of his mouth. Yearning pours through me like molten lava and I'm fused to him, inside and out, as a wellspring of emotion overwhelms me.

"Who told you otherwise?" The sad tone that escapes between his lips isn't sad for me. Carrying a distinct sound of disapproval, he's correcting the distant critic who put it out there, the one who planted the seed of inadequacy inside me.

The guy who made me feel like I wasn't enough – because I was a little too much.

"They were *wrong*." The emphasis on the last word makes me shudder.

"Perfect and ripe and warm," he whispers, making me melt more.

The feel of his tanned skin under my own palms, how his eyes seem so interested and captivated, the play of his words on those lips as he misses me and says more that I can't really understand because oh—*oh!*—now he moves in a pattern that takes me to places where words are mere formalities.

Where sensation is the language of choice.

One finger trails a line between my breasts and he plants a kiss in the valley. "You're everything I want," he whispers, tension in his voice stretching his words out as he begins his own tipping point. He takes one pebbled nipple in his mouth and the rush of warm wetness makes me clench, which in turn makes him groan.

No words. The leather seat presses against my knees and he brushes my hair away from my face, tucking it behind an ear with such precision as he tongues my breast and makes me stop. Stop thinking, stop wiggling, stop the world—stop *time*, because I am everything and nothing in his arms.

My own body moves in long, even strokes against his, and then without warning he's above me, out of me, leaving me with a hollow ache that cries out for more. Declan's arm wraps around my waist and he spins me effortlessly under him, the limo seat so wide we can fit comfortably, our thighs slick with sweat and more, his face filled with passion and a tantalizing seriousness that brings back a handful of words.

"You're beautiful, too," I whisper, looking up at him as anticipation is poised between us in that timeless moment before we break through the invisible wall. The wall that separates every couple before they knowingly – *willfully* – breach it to connect two separate beings, making one flesh, one desire, one need.

One climax. Giving yourself to another person is one thing. Truly letting go as you lose yourself in them is quite another.

"I didn't know there were men like you out there," I add, reaching up to push a lock of hair out of his face. He's so intense, so purely centered on me, eyes alive and fully in the moment. We're on a threshold, and I have so much bursting inside me that I want to say.

"You make me feel like it's okay to be me, Declan. No one's ever done that before." Our breath mingles in the small space between us, my legs tightening around him, my body and heart wanting to be as close as possible. I'd have to crawl inside him to be any closer, and I'm shaking with an all-consuming force that is so much more than anything I've felt.

"I wouldn't want you to be anyone else, Shannon."

I smile wide as he drives home inside me, his face dipped down to kiss me, his mouth fire and ice as he thrusts, my body filled with a kind of madness that makes me seek release at the same time that I can't help but cling to him.

His hands rest on my waist as he tightens, his face hot over mine, our bodies half clothed. This feels so illicit, so naughty, and as the limo comes to a pause at a stoplight a massive plume of boldness blooms in me.

This is who I am. Declan is who I want. His face shifts as he pushes over and over, my legs shaking and my hands seeking whatever skin he has exposed, the connection morphing into something so illicitly primal.

And when he leans down, still in control, his hand between my legs and giving the slightest butterfly touch where I need it most, I utter his name in a fevered moan, my climax hitting without reservation, all restraint gone, my mouth full of whispers and groans, my fingers digging into his shoulders as he tells me to come, to come, to *come*.

I do.

He joins me, torso and chest tense and hands digging into the leather seat on either side of me, my legs wrapped around his waist, his murmurs in my ear as he bites the lobe and shudders like he's captivated by a series of prayers to a god I can believe in. The air around us is hot and spicy, like woman and man mingling together, the scent of sex and sweat and perfume and cologne burning into my brain.

This is the scent of mind-blowing sex. Yankee Candle needs to patent it.

"You," he says with a hiss, pulling out of me and turning around. He ties off the condom and throws it discreetly in a small trash can with a little swish lid that makes me laugh. I don't know why. The giggles descend on me and I cannot stop.

"That's a first," he says.

"Sex in a limo?" I gasp between chuckles.

He gets a surprisingly sheepish look on his face. "Uh, no," he says slowly. But not apologetically.

If this awkward turn of conversation is supposed to spoil the mood, it doesn't. I just laugh even more. Absurdity makes me laugh. Having sex for the first time in a year makes me giggle. Fucking Declan in the back of a limo makes me sputter.

"What's a first, then?"

"A woman overcome with giggles after sleeping with me. Most don't find it so…comedic."

"I just had sex in a limo," I explain.

"You know what comes next?" he says as he pulls up his pants and snaps and zips up. I realize I am completely naked from the waist up and scramble to find my shirt, unable to think. Naked! In a limo! With Hot Guy! Laughing!

"What?" I ask as I shove my arms into my sleeves and pull the shirt over my head. Wait. Where's my bra? Oh. There it is. Hanging on the door handle, one strap wrapped around the gleaming metal, the other on the neck of a crystal decanter of something amber, lounging lazily.

"Love in a helicopter."

Chapter Six

"Is that a promise or a threat?" I ask as my head shoots through the neck of my shirt, my hair caught under it. I'm sweaty and feel like I've just climbed Mt. Declan, legs aching and body buzzing. But *ahhh*, the summit was damn nice, and the view...

"Both." He laughs and rides his hand up over my thigh.

"I like both." I close my eyes, trying not to cringe as I feel him brush against my decidedly not-smooth leg.

He senses the change in me and caresses my jaw with his fingers, turning my eyes to him. "What is it?"

This is the moment when every woman balances between saying "fine" and telling the truth. I'm sitting in a limousine with a man who holds more power than two hundred of me combined, and all I can think about are my stubbly shins.

The divided mind turns me in two distinct directions:

He's different. Real and genuine. Go with it.
and
He's about as interested in the truth as he is in

going to CVS to buy you a pack of tampons.

I go for the former, because the cocky grin he's giving me right now is so authentic that it feels right to be honest and open, vulnerable and real, and to stop worrying about what I think he's thinking.

How about I try just saying what I think?

Deep breath. Deep breath. The car lurches forward and his hand tightens on my thigh, his other arm snaking around me protectively. I nestle in and say:

"I wasn't exactly prepared for a date." I run my own hand against my legs and say, "*Skritch skritch skritch*." And then I close my eyes and wish for a tornado to appear and take me away so I can wake up and realize this is all a dream. Plus the ruby shoes would be a nice addition to my wardrobe.

I can't believe I just said that. Skritch? What am I, an animated character from *Ice Age*?

"Sound effects?" His booming laugh fills the car. Bright lights dot the horizon as the sun nearly finishes setting, and I realize we're at a small airport. "You're giving me sound effects?"

He runs his hand along my leg and up between my legs. A rush of heat, and yet more arousal fills me. How can I want more?

"I like sound effects," he adds, "but the ones you made a few minutes ago were far superior."

"I—" My lips turn to liquid, like he just shot me with ten times my weight in Novocaine.

"If I want a smooth woman, I'll put you in my clawfoot tub at home and shave you myself," he says.

Blink.

"I'll run you a hot bath, undress you with my own hands, soap you up and make you com—" He licks his lips and looks me up and down, then continues. "—fortable. And that's a promise," he adds, leaning down for a deep kiss. I can imagine the scene; his eyes show it to me.

The car comes to a slow stop and the engine goes silent. I can't speak. Can't move. Can't think. I'm one big, throbbing hormone.

Declan pulls away and points out the window to a helicopter. A sleek black machine that looks like something out of a movie, like the insect version of a Transformer.

"What are you, Batman?" I ask as words return to me, marveling at all this. A headphoned pilot is at the controls, and the blades aren't moving. Lights blink and Declan steps out of the limo, waving to the driver, who climbs back in the front seat.

I step out on legs that feel strong and well used. The copter blades start a slow circle and sound revs up.

"I wish. But you'll have to settle for plain old Declan," he shouts.

"You're anything but 'plain,'" I call back.

Cupping a hand over his ear, he shakes his head. He didn't hear me. That's okay, though, because he doesn't need to.

The ground feels springy under my feet as I hold my hair in one hand to keep it from whipping around my face as the helicopter blades rotate faster. The wind the machine creates is magical, the contraption about to elevate us into the air, high above the city. I have no idea where Declan is taking me and I don't care. My body throbs and I'm sore from that amazing encounter in the limo, but I get the distinct sense that *that*?

That was only the beginning.

Love in a helicopter? No way. The pilot gives me a sharp nod, the engines roaring so loud I can't hear a thing. Declan offers me headphones and I put them on, muting the *chuk chuk chuk* sound.

"Welcome aboard, Ms. Jacoby," says a new-to-me voice. The pilot raises his hand with a wave.

"That's Joel," Declan's voice explains, crackling over a static-y connection. He points to a little knob on his own headset and I realize it's the volume control. I fiddle with mine and get the sound to the right level. Speaking in a normal voice is all that's needed.

Joel speaks a bunch of Flight Language to some sort of tower personnel. He might as well be casting a spell or getting directions to Hogwarts. The words and numbers make no sense to me, but I'm in awe of it anyhow. That a human being can learn how to successfully navigate a machine like this, not only through space but through three-dimensional space, is amazing.

Driving a car on the ground is hard enough, but to know which direction you're going and to keep track of where you are vertically? It's like rubbing your tummy, patting your head, and playing Farmville while singing "The Star-Spangled Banner" at the same time.

And this is why I never became a pilot. That, and failing Physics 101. Pesky detail.

Declan's speaking in code with Joel, his hip digging deep into mine as we cram next to each other on the helicopter. He closes the door and the sound of the blades changes. It's like someone shoved a feather pillow over them. The helicopter begins to jostle and I dig my fingers into his thigh.

He smiles at me, all stubble and dimples and bright irises. A reassuring arm wraps around me. "Takeoff is always hardest," he says.

"I'll bet you say that to all the girls."

Joel makes a snorting sound, then cuts his mic. Declan shoots him an annoyed look, but returns his attention to me. "I've never taken a woman in my chopper before. Not on a date."

"Is that what you call this?" I can't stop touching him. My hand goes to the collar of his shirt, where a smattering of dark hair covers his collarbone. I want to lick him. Taste him. Nestle my cheek against his chest and hear his heartbeat. I want him in me again, the feel of his release, of his trust to give in to me.

Divergence is turning my life into something unrecognizable. A few weeks ago I knew what to expect from your average day. No, I couldn't plan it meticulously, no matter how hard I tried, but a certain contentment made each week pretty predictable. Settled. Relatively comfortable, if a bit lonely. Get up, have coffee, go to work, do mystery shops, prepare presentations, come home to Chuckles, hang with Amy and Amanda.

Lather, rinse, repeat.

Drive my junky car. Have dinner at Mom and Dad's. Overthink and overplan everything, then obsess about my tendency to overthink and overplan.

A billionaire player like Declan was, most definitely, not part of any plan. Not even part of my fantasies, which had taken a bizarre turn toward the superhero realm. If you can't have a superman, you might as well get off on dreams of threesomes with Iron Man and Loki.

My Batman joke really was just a joke, though.

Declan is better than the Avengers and the X-Men combined. As I stroke the fine weave of his wool suit pants, his thigh shifts under my measured touch. Rippled steel bands react under my palm, the soft inner thigh flesh yielding the tiniest bit as I grasp him, feel his response. He inhales slowly and rests his chin on the top of my head, closing his eyes.

He's enjoying this. Letting me explore him, confirm he's real and under my inventory. Here's his forearm. There's his biceps. And the chest is right here. The scruff on his cheek makes contact with my cheekbone and I soften into him. Our bodies fit beautifully together. We fit together.

We.

We can't say a word to each other right now unless we want the pilot to hear, so we sit in silence. His hands mimic mine, soon finding my curves and valleys, swells and peaks. The way he touches me makes me feel desired. Appreciated. Not just wanted, because anyone can be wanted.

He makes me feel *cherished.*

"Check out the Red Sox game," he says, pointing to the well-lit Fenway Park. It's an early game for the season. Everyone seems so tiny, so insignificant, and yet thousands—tens of thousands —of people are all congregated to watch the game, to party, to be one with the energy of the crowd.

For a split second, I wish Amanda were here. Sex in a limo with a near-billionaire! And a hot man who looks like a *Men's Health* cover model. Watching a Red Sox game from above, flying over the gleaming city lights.

Me—*Shannon*—with Declan McCormick.

And then…my own mind does a 180-degree turn. Sometimes the clearest moments come when you least expect them, and this is one of those times.

You can't believe it because you won't let yourself believe it. Let go of your own self as an obstacle and imagine how much more you could do and be.

And be cherished.

Tears threaten the inner corners of my eyes. My throat aches with a sickly, bitter taste. I lean in to Declan and press my ear against his heart, the fine cloth of his shirt cool until my face warms it. A tear mars the perfect whiteness of his shirt and I don't care.

Thu-thump. Thu-thump. Thu-thump. Steady and strong, his heart continues at its regular pace. I wonder if he's always like this. So calm, so confident. Without being smarmy or a blowhard, Declan manages to embody so many qualities I've wanted in a man, but thought were mythical.

He's nothing like my own father, who is a sweet, non-judgmental man. But Dad isn't the dominant type. I've never seen him move through life making split-second decisions and assessments of character and behavior and filtering a person in or out based on their response. Dad doesn't walk into a room with a feeling of command. He's many wonderful things, but Jason Jacoby is anything but the leader of a pack.

And that's okay. Really. Because I can love my dad but want a man for myself who is completely different.

"We're almost there," Declan says, pointing through the window at the scattered lights below. I'm so deep in my thoughts that somehow I manage to forget to look outside, to see the show unfolding beneath us. Complete darkness has descended over the city; it's a moonless night, so up here in the sky, the air has a whiff of intrigue to it. Without the bright white orb in the sky to shepherd us, the chopper's movements feel more than a little surreal, like riding Space Mountain at Disney, except there is no enclosed building, no track, no line.

We move down, more of the city rolling out before our eyes. A long patch of nothingness spills into view suddenly. The copter shifts downward and we're flying fast over water. Declan kisses my ear and I see the white caps of waves cresting, my body drained. I'm tired and spent, yet wired and excited.

It's not from the copter ride.

It's from knowing there're so much more to come.

Joel says a bunch of numbers and phrases again, then suddenly we're hovering a few feet above the ground on a tiny island, a tall building brightly lit right next to us. The flight itself was fast, so fast we must be on one of the Boston Harbor islands. I can't tell which one. The tall, lit building is a lighthouse, the old kind. The lighthouse's beacon faces out to sea and a small golf cart is parked next to the structure.

"Powering down," Joel explains. I sit in place, the copter's vibrations making my skin tingle. I'm parched, and just as the last *snick* sound from the blades' rotation makes its final sigh, my stomach growls louder than a zombie bear that stumbled across a bunch of fresh raccoon brains.

"Hungry?"

"Starving."

Declan has a satisfied look on his face, as if he's hiding something he's quite proud of. "Good. You'll like what's coming next."

As long as it's me, I think. He gives me a look that says he's read my mind.

I'm about as graceful as a three-legged elephant with arthritis as I climb out of the helicopter, managing somehow to step on Declan's foot and elbow him in the abs as he helps me down. Joel gives us a thumbs-up and walks away as Declan takes my elbow and escorts me to a small door at the base of the lighthouse.

"I assume we're still in the United States?" I ask. "Because I left my passport at home."

"Glad to hear you have one," he says as he opens the tattered wood door, the paint worn down, the old dark oak underneath poking through under white paint as faded as old bones left out in the sun for too many summers. A narrow set of stairs, all made of concrete from a time when I imagine puritans hand-mixed it, curls up to the sky in a dizzying spiral. I inhale the scent of sea salt and centuries.

His words warm me, though. Where could we go? Where would he take me? Not that it matters, as long as I'm with him. He hinted about New Zealand last week, but I thought he'd been joking.

I guess not. My neck hurts from staring straight up, the lighthouse's peak blocked by a ceiling.

"What is this place?" I ask. I can see the stairs curve up at the top and stop.

"I wanted to take you somewhere you've never been. Finding a restaurant that a mystery shopper has never eaten in or evaluated is a daunting task. But I think I've risen to the occasion." His hand on the small of my back pushes gently so that I go inside, my shoes scraping against old stone.

The main door clicks shut and echoes up, the sound carrying to the heavens.

"I think you've succeeded," I whisper. My voice reverberates. I shiver involuntarily, and Declan's arm is around me instantly, pulling me to his warmth.

"You scared?" He's amused.

"No," I protest. "It's just a little cold. And dark." Flickering gas lamps dot the path upwards, like something out of a Gothic novel. Declan clearly has a thing for these sorts of places. The walls remind me of a mausoleum without the names and dates etched in the front-facing stones.

"Don't worry," he says, pulling back and gesturing for me to go first up the stairs. "The manacles on the torture chamber are lined with a nice, thick sherpa fleece."

Chapter Seven

I halt so fast his front slams into my ass. I can feel *exactly* how he's risen to the occasion.

"Huh?"

"That was a joke."

I turn and face him. His lips are twitching around a poorly contained look of amusement.

"Look here, buddy," I say, poking my finger against his perfect chest. "This isn't like one of those books where the billionaire steals the poor, underpaid intern away from her horrible life and they discover a mutually beneficial BDSM lifestyle, m'kay?"

He pretends to be crestfallen. "Oh. Okay. Then I'll just call Joel and we'll take you home." He reaches into his back pocket for his phone and fake dials. I can see he's actually on ESPN and checking scores. The Red Sox are playing at Fenway right now. I know that because we flew over them, and that fact makes the entire night seem so surreal.

Seem? I t *is* surreal. Magical. A little too perfect.

My stomach growls in protest. "What about dinner?" I ignore him and start walking up the stairs. There's no railing, so I cling to the stones with splayed palms, thanking God I'm not wearing high heels.

"Nice view," he says, suspiciously close behind me. A warm hand slides up between my thighs. "Here, let me lend you a hand."

"That hand isn't helping." His fingers slide under my already-soaked panties and he gives me the slightest touch against my wetness. We pause and I cling to the wall with even weaker legs.

"Really?" he murmurs against the back of my neck. "It seems to be making things much... smoother."

"You're slick."

"Actually," he says, "you're the one who's slick." As tantalizing as being felt up on the stairs is, there's a very real danger that we will roll down the stone steps and end up in the hospital again and I, for one, cannot emotionally handle two dates in a row ending with an Explanation of Benefits form and an ER co-pay.

"Let's get upstairs and see what you have for me."

He takes my hand and puts it on his fly.

"That's not quite what I meant, Declan."

He glides past me, making sure to press every inch of his chiseled self against my own soft curves, taking the steps up carefully until his ass is in my face. It's a fabulous view.

"Normally I'd say 'ladies first,' but right now you're procrastinating, so—"

"You're groping me on the stairs and making it so I can't even walk! How is that procrastinating?"

76

I'm talking to air, though, because by the time I say that, he's halfway to the top, bounding up like this is part of *The Amazing Race* and he's on the annoying team that's always way ahead of everyone else because they're in good shape and all that unfair crap.

So I trek my way up, one frightening stair at a time. My hand brushes against something soft on the stones and I scream.

"What's wrong?" he calls down.

If I confess, he'll just make fun of me. Or, worse, come back here and drive me wild with those fingers and we'll tumble down the stairs to our deaths. No one would find us for days. We would be the lead story on New England Cable News for weeks.

Billionaire Meets Death with Klutzy Woman. News at eleven.

I force myself to take the stairs at a faster clip. By the time I climb the equivalent of three stories, my quads are screaming.

Screaming to be wrapped around his hips.

The most delicious scent tickles my nose as I make the final turn up to the top of the stairs, Declan standing there, holding open a small door. I have to duck to enter. Oregano and rosemary and something else fill the air, and as I come to a full standing position I'm greeted by a scene out of a dream.

Tall, sculpted windows arch high toward a flat ceiling, with the ocean surrounding us in a 360-degree spin that is beyond breathtaking. The room is just beneath what I assume is the lighthouse's warning light, because an arch of glow comes from above at regular intervals, making this room ethereal and supernatural, as if Declan had conjured it with magic.

The actual room has a small soapstone stove with a fire burning in it, which helps, because the air is chilled this high up and far out into the harbor. Two large L-shaped sofas ring the wood stove, and a series of blown-glass lamps dangle from the ceiling in muted earth tones and adobe. Thick Persian rugs cover the well-worn wood of the floor, wide pine flooring hearkening back to a very different time.

And a small table for two with candles in large crab buckets filled with seashells is the source of the incredible smell that makes my mouth water and my stomach beg for mercy.

Declan has that effect on me, too, but right now I am all about the meal. I need some calories. Sustenance. Protein, because one of those sofas is so big and covered with a small Matterhorn of pillows, and the entire room is like a woman's idea of the perfect sex den.

Which it is.

His arm sweeping out in a welcoming gesture, he invites me to sit at the table. I see a plate full of chocolate-covered strawberries, cheese, and a bottle of white wine.

"You know me well."

"I want to know you better." Declan pulls out the chair and I sit, scooching in, my hand reaching for one of the strawberries without thinking. The bite is sweet and juicy, the chocolate smooth and creamy, and this time, there are no bees to ruin my mouthgasm.

Declan sits across from me and leans back, his hands at his navel, eyes piercing. "You come here often?" he asks.

"Nice pickup line," I mumble through a mouth full of awesome. I swallow and look right back at him. "But you should know I'm a sure thing."

His throaty laugh makes me tingle in all the right places. Again? *Again?* Confession time: I've never had sex twice in one night with a guy. Given a blow job and had sex? Yes. But actual *sex* sex twice in the same night? Nope. I'm at a loss here, frankly. We, um, did the deed. Now we're eating dinner. This sumptuous room is designed for nothing but rolling in the sheets.

Or lack of sheets. Naked on that soft, velvety couch. Or the rug. Or just…naked. Anywhere. My eyes drift to the glass walls facing the ocean, the sound of waves lapping against the island's shores like the blood pounding through me. Imagine making love while looking out into the expansiveness of—

"You're deep in thought." Declan's pouring two glasses of wine and I didn't even notice him stand and uncork the bottle. It's getting hot in here. I finish my strawberry and smile at him, reaching for the wine.

Which I promptly drink in a series of gulps that would make any NBA player on a time-out proud.

"This is unbelievable, Declan," I say, looking around. "How did you find this? Is it a restaurant? It doesn't look like one."

"It's ours for tonight."

"That's it? C'mon. Explain."

He smiles. "Okay. I donate money to a historical preservation society that works on buying and restoring lighthouses. This one isn't in danger, but plenty of others are. I know someone who knows someone who sacrificed a few small animals to give me access to this place. It's the only lighthouse within a short helicopter ride from Boston. I hired a few people to outfit the place to my specifications and...here we are."

"I think that's the most you've ever said to me in one breath."

He shrugs. "You insisted."

"Why?"

"Why did you insist?"

"No. I mean, why all this?" I throw my hands up. "This. You didn't need to do this for me."

"I didn't need to. I want to."

"Why?"

"For the same reason you're here."

Letting go of this nagging "why me" voice is harder than I thought. I imagine Chuckles looking at me with disapproval, shaking his head. The man just made love to me in a limo, for goodness' sake. Of course he wants me. Of course he likes me. At the rate I'm going, I'll ruin this, so—

Let

80

It

Go

Great. Now I have the theme song from *Frozen* stuck in my head forever. Yeah. Sure. Try making love with that pinging through your brain. Disney characters are only aphrodisiacs for people who troll FetLife.

Declan's eyes have narrowed and he's watching me. "You really do wear your emotions on your face."

"And in my hands," I add, flailing them. He's been wearing his suit jacket this whole time—even when we were doing the nasty back in the limo—and now he slips out of it, stretching the fabric across the back of a cloth-covered dining chair that's primly tied with a neat bow.

His shoulder muscles ripple with movement under his shirt and I realize I've never seen him naked. Never even seen him shirtless. My breath comes in sudden halts as it hits me that I'm really here. Mr. Grey Suit is in front of me in an intimate, romantic setting he created for me, and this is my real life.

He unbuttons the cuffs of his shirt and rolls them up. I'm hypnotized. I can't stop watching as his deft fingers go through the motions like a performance, his eyes tilted down and watching what he's doing, making himself comfortable.

He's spent so much time thinking about my comfort. Focused on me. My eyes eat him up, enjoying not just the view but the intimacy of this moment. So simple. So ordinary. Just a man on a date in a new relationship, rolling up his sleeves after a long day at the office, waiting to sink into a lovely dinner and some nice sexy time.

Except he's flown across countless time zones, interrupted my pseudo-date with my ignorant ex, had his way with me in a limo, flown me in a helicopter to a remote island, and now he has me (voluntarily) trapped on a remote island where anything could happen.

So not ordinary.

"Enjoying yourself?" His voice is warm milk and burnt sugar and rum-soaked ladyfingers with hot fudge sauce and an invitation to spend a weekend on Martha's Vineyard on the beach without clothes or other people.

"I really like what I see." It helps that I just felt his abs underneath me and they roll like Ben Wa balls, sleek, sexy and hypnotically solid.

"Me, too." He reaches for my hand and takes a long, slow sip of his wine. My own gulp earlier is kicking in, loosening me, making me want to run my legs against silk sheets and the soft strands of his leg hair, imagining his naked body and his own happy trail leading down...

I don't have to imagine it, though, do I? I'm about to live it.

Without comment or affect, Declan lifts the covers off our plates, revealing lobster and steak. "I hope you're not allergic to shellfish," he says dryly.

"No, thank God. I love lobster." We smile at each other, and something's different. I face it head on.

"Speaking of allergies, thank you. I didn't know about your brother."

"Of course you didn't. But now you do." He picks up his silverware with hands that are steady. Mine are shaking like a four-year-old with a pogo stick on Christmas morning.

"Good for me, then, that you came prepared."

He pauses mid-bite. "Yes," is all he says, then continues eating. The lights above us go round and round, giving the room a hypnotic glow.

"How does Andrew handle it?" I take a bite and let my words hang there. Declan's quiet, finishing his food, and I get the sense that he doesn't want to talk about this, but I do. There's no way I'm going to act like it never happened.

"Handle being so allergic?"

"No, handle being the Green Lantern."

He smiles. "Touché. Okay, he handles it by carefully orchestrating a life where he's never near a wasp."

I laugh. Declan pours another glass of wine for me. I nod my thanks and he sets the bottle down, conspicuously not filling his own glass.

"Impossible."

His eyebrows go up in mirth. "No, it's quite possible. He has drivers who meet him in underground parking garages, flies only at night in the cooler temperatures for that twenty-foot walk on private tarmacs to the company jet, and exercises indoors."

"He must be paler than a vampire." Then again, so's my belly. It hasn't seen sunlight since

Kristen Stewart smiled.

"Tanning booths and vitamin D supplements cover that."

I'm chewing a glorious piece of lobster as his words sink in. "You're joking."

He swallows his own bite and finishes his wine. "I'm completely serious. It's how he copes."

I'm stunned. The allergists over the years have cautioned me to take measures that reduce my risk, but no one's ever suggested such extremes. "Were his stings that bad?"

"He's only been stung once."

"Once?"

"And his throat closed up."

"Oof. That's really rare. You don't normally have a reaction that bad for the first time you're stung."

"Bad enough that he lost consciousness. We got him to the ER in time." I can tell he really, really doesn't want to talk about this, but it's calming me. Centering me. Hearing him talk about his own experiences and his brother's allergies makes me feel less like an oddity.

"Your mother and father must have freaked."

"Mom was dead by then." His face is a stone mask. My heart squeezes.

"Oh." What the hell can I say after that? Shoving a mouthful of perfectly done filet is the only way to respond. Declan pours himself another glass of wine, filling it within a half-inch of the rim, then empties the rest of the bottle into my glass.

Neither of us has to drive, so why not?

He studies me, taking liberal sips of his wine, then puts the glass down and reaches for my free hand. I'm slowing down, full of delectable food, wired and aroused.

"You're worried I can't handle the bee thing." It's not a question. And he's mostly right.

I take a moment to think about this before answering. "No. Not quite." He gives me a skeptical look. "It's more that you handled it so well. Precisely perfect. The last time I was stung I was with Steve, who ran away in a panic and screamed so much the EMTs who arrived after I called 911 thought *he* was the bee sting victim. Delayed my treatment."

Declan's face goes tight and angry. "Not only is he an asshole, he's a dangerous little shit. Leaving you in a medical crisis." With a hand so tight I'm afraid he'll shatter his wine goblet, he grabs the wine and drinks it all down in a series of fast gulps that make his neck stretch, muscles on display.

"You learn a lot about people in a crisis."

Chapter Eight

My words hang there as he stares at me a few beats longer than normal. My heart is throbbing about two feet lower on my body, our eyes connecting for seconds longer than they should, the air warm and charged.

"You learn everything you need to know," he declares.

"Then you now know that I will turn you into a Viagra eater in a crisis."

He wants to laugh but doesn't let himself. "I think, in a true emergency, that you click out of this insecure mode you live in and the core person inside picks up."

I lean forward on my elbow, pushing my plate away, and reach for my wine. Two sips later and I ask, "Tell me more about this core." My actual core pulses from down below, wanting him to touch it. I could give him GPS coordinates at this point. Hell, I could take my leftover food on my plate and create a food sculpture map to help him.

"You first. Tell me what you think about me." What guy does this? HUH?

"What I think about you? You're a superman, Declan. You're Hot Guy. I'm Toilet Girl. I'm wondering why"—I gesture around the room—"you picked me."

"*Tsk tsk*," he chides. "That's not what I asked."

"Okay, what I think about you."

"What you think about me. Not what you think about 'Declan McCormick.'" Yes, he uses finger quotes. "What you think about *me*." His eyes are soulful. Serious. Contemplative and evaluative. He's asking a very different question in those eyes than he's saying with his mouth.

"You. Just…you. Not the image. The man."

His lids close and he lets out a long sigh. "Yes."

"I think you're an enigma because I don't know you that well." His eyes fly open. "And yet I feel like I've known your forever." He reaches for my hand and I grasp his, hard.

"I feel the closest I've ever felt to being *myself* when I'm with you. Whoever that is. You don't judge me. You don't shame me or act like I'm the outsider in everything. You don't use sarcasm like it's a tool or a weapon, and you speak so plainly and clearly it's like you've invented a new language."

The room goes still. The lighthouse light stops. We're lit by candle and the flicker makes shadows shimmer across his face in a pattern that burns into my memory as it unfolds. I will never forget this moment until the day I die, which will hopefully be when we are in our nineties, in bed after making love, and holding hands.

"You're this bad-boy billionaire—" He starts to protest and I hold up a hand, brushing my fingers against his lips. "That's what your image says. Billionaire. You're the jet-setting Boston Magazine society pages poster boy whose father built a crazy-massive empire. You're one of the Bachelor Brothers everyone talks about. You and Andrew and Terrance are all over the local blogs, the free grocery-store newspapers, the *Boston Globe*, all the magazines. Women like Jessica Coffin want to marry you and have posh little babies and host Beacon Hill ballroom parties in your townhomes with the warped eighteenth century glass windows. The ones the rest of us only see from the outside in the summer when we can scrape together enough money to afford to take a long ride on a Duck Tour."

He chuckles against my hand, then kisses my palm, pressing it against his face.

"Go on."

"You want more?"

"Hell yes, I want more."

"No." His eyes widen a bit with surprise. I've challenged him. He doesn't smile, but the eyes stay intrigued. "Your turn," I add.

A long pause. Too long. The room feels so small, so warm as I'm under his scrutiny, my request feeling like a gauntlet thrown on the ground too hard.

And then:

"You make me think about my life beyond the date, the kiss, the sex, the ride home."

He stands abruptly, eyes filled with more emotion that I can't interpret. In a flash, I'm in his arms, his mouth on mine, the taste of wine on his lips, his tongue, making my head spin even more. My hands slip around his waist and untuck his shirt, reaching up to feel his bare skin.

Declan pulls back, our mouths an inch from each other. "When I look at you I can see my future roll out in one long laugh, like a red carpet of fun and intelligence and hope. A ripple of joy that stretches into the horizon until it disappears. Not because it ceases to exist, but because it's infinite."

My heart presses directly against his, and the two beat in sync. Our foreheads touch and his eyes blur as my vision goes hazy. I close my eyes, his words, oh, those words...

"I know who I am in the world, Shannon. I don't need you to define me. What I need from you is what I can't find on my own. And right here"—he lifts my chin, his eyes loving and warm—"right here." His hand slides between us and settles on my heart. "Is where you redefine me."

He kisses me gently.

A slow shake of his head makes me blink over and over, signals confusing and overwhelming. My knees tingle and his arms are the only thing pinning me to earth. "I don't talk like this with the women I date. I'm not even quite sure where these words are coming from." He smiles like he's asking me to translate, but my heart is on edge, waiting for me. "My heart, I guess."

Mine stands up like it's doing the wave in a giant stadium filled with all the heartbreak I've experienced until now. And yes, it feels like it fills a stadium.

"I don't feel this way with the women I date. But you're nothing like the typical women in my life, and this is anything but a typical relationship."

Our kiss deepens and I reach down, cupping his tight ass. Which buzzes suddenly. I jump and move my hand away.

He sighs. "I've been ignoring that for the past twenty minutes, but…"

I pull the phone out of his back pocket and give him an extra squeeze. He groans. I shrug. He looks at his phone and groans extra loud.

"Damn it. I have to call Grace."

"I understand. She's the 'Other Woman.'" My turn to use finger quotes. They feel as stupid as they seem.

He cocks one eyebrow and stares me down.

"I'm joking."

"I know you are, because Grace is old enough to be my grandmother and is married to a rugby player."

I laugh. "He'd kill you if you made a move."

"She."

"She what?"

"Grace's wife. Seventy-three-year-old female rugby player."

Leaving me with that interesting tidbit, he turns away and speaks into the phone. I take the opportunity to check my own phone.

Twenty-seven messages. Nine from Steve:

What the hell, Shannon?
He's such an asshole.

Are you safe?
I think he's an emotional abuser.
Your car's still here.
Should I call the police?
I texted your mother.
Thank him for paying.
Ask him what he thinks about Canford Industries and whether it's a good stock buy.

Delete. I repeat it nine times. Go ahead, Steve. Call the police. The fact that you texted my mother means…

Yep.

Nine messages from her:

You ditched Steve for Declan? Good girl. Aim higher. Shall I start booking a spring 2015 spot at Farmington?

I don't even read the other eight. Delete times nine.

Eight from Amanda:

Your mother is texting me. You ditched Steve?
Is Declan being emotionally abusive? Steve's saying yes.
Steve is on Twitter creating hashtags about you.

Huh? I stop reading and call her, furious.

"What the hell is going on?" I hiss into the phone. Declan's back is still turned, his shirt tail hanging out over that hot, tight ass I just had in my hands. Now I'm spewing invective at my best friend about my arrogant ex. Something is very wrong with this picture. The candles still burn, the room is still filled with sex and promise, and I'm—venting about *Steve*?

"Steve's been calling and texting your mom and me about how Declan appeared and made you leave. How scared and vulnerable you looked. How he thinks you're being emotionally abused."

I just had the most mind-blowing sex of my life while straddling Declan in a limo and I have to deal with an ex who is acting like a middle school gossip girl?

"He WHAT?" I ask. A little too loudly, too, because Declan frowns and walks toward me.

"What's wrong?" Declan asks. I can't wiggle out of this one.

"Nothing," I say with a chirp. I'm turning into Amanda. There's no way I'm telling her what Declan just said to me, his heartfelt confession, because I can't even wrap my head and heart around the words. He said everything I feel, except with clarity. When I think the same words they just come out like unintelligible babble. "Just a...work problem."

"Not with an Anterdec property?"

"No, no...just a pest control issue," I hiss. I motion for him to go back to his call and suddenly, the room feels cold. Broken. Lost.

Or maybe it's just me.

I hear a decidedly masculine voice on the other

end of Declan's call, the dissonance between my assumption it was Grace and the male voice confusing. "Declan?" the voice says. "Just because you don't like what I have to say about her doesn't mean you should ignore me."

I know that voice. It's James, his father.

Declan frowns at his screen and shows me his back. Hmmm. "Her"? Does his father not like me? Or are they talking about some other woman? Of course they are. I'm being silly and self-centered. Why would James McCormick 1) not like me? That's akin to not liking a golden retriever. I'm the epitome of nice and 2) even bother with me. He only noticed me because Declan pointed me out in that business meeting a few weeks ago, and almost bailed on a business trip to swing by my office, and saved my life...

Hmmm.

"Steve's crazy, Shannon, and we know it. Don't worry. Your mom thinks you're a feminist hero, though, for going on one date and leaving with another guy." Amanda's voice slices through my rapid-fire thoughts.

"I wasn't on a date with Steve! I'd rather get a Brazilian wax with battery acid."

"Ouch," she says in unison with Declan, who is now off the phone and behind me, all heat and muscle bearing down, moving with a slight rhythm that tells me exactly what—and who—is coming next.

"Gotta go, Amanda. We're in a lighthouse in the harbor and Declan's about to—"

Click.

"About to…?" He kisses my shoulder, taking the phone out of my hand as his thumb presses the "Power" button. His chest is hot against my back and as he leans around me to set down my phone on the table, I realize his shirt's unbuttoned. Bare skin warms my cotton shirt and he turns me to face him.

I look at the L-shaped couches across the room, the flicker of fire in the glass door of the wood stove making the velvet seem so soft, so welcoming.

Like Declan's hands as he lifts my shirt for what feels like the umpteenth time this evening.

"You," he says with a growl as he reveals my bra, "are so hot."

"I'm Toilet Girl."

"You're Hot Girl."

"That's *your* title."

"I'm Hot Girl?" He takes my hand and puts it at his waistband as he undoes his belt. He has a point.

"I retract that statement."

"This isn't a newspaper article. You're not a reporter." His voice holds a smile. "Unless you're undercover and investigating me."

"I'm only dating you for the account," I joke. "Nothing more. No Woodward and Bernstein. No deep cover."

"If you're only dating me for the account, then you nailed it two dates ago," he whispers as he unclasps my bra. The shiver that runs through me vibrates into the scarred wood floor, carrying out into the ocean's waves, triggering a tsunami somewhere in the Azores islands.

"Then why am I here?"

His mouth stops me from saying more, slanting against mine, his arms strong and lifting me to tiptoes. My bare breasts press against the heat of his pecs and the push of his abs against my belly makes me feel more intimate than when he was inside me, in the limo.

"Let me show you exactly why you're here, Shannon."

And he does.

.

Chapter Nine

"Your medical emergency made the local Patch news!" Mom shouts from the kitchen. Mom begged and begged and begged and guilted and blackmailed me into coming to one of her yoga classes, and then she snuck into my phone and texted Declan, pretending to be me, and he's here.

Here. Standing in my childhood home drinking orange spice tea and wearing workout clothes that make me feel feral.

"Great. Just what we need. Notoriety from a news site that covers misspelled store signs and duck crossings with as much space as they cover fatal car accidents and government corruption," Declan mutters.

"What did they say, Mom?" I ask, forcing myself to be polite. I'm drinking chamomile tea and it's not relaxing me. You could pump Zen Tea into me via IV and it wouldn't work. My heart is the sound of one hand clapping, flailing in the wind, trying to find something to rest against.

Watching Declan sit on our sunken sofa, perched with perfect posture and powerful legs encased in lycra stretch fabric, confuses the hell out of the wiring in my brain.

"And Jessica Coffin mentioned you!"

Declan groans, then covers it with a sip. His eyes take in the room. Mom has a thing for thrift shopping, even though Dad complains that we can afford to buy new, as long as it's at a discount warehouse. Born and raised in New England, Mom's Yankee sensibilities tell her she can't dare to buy a new dresser even though she spends $60 a week on mani-pedis. The incongruity has been long pointed out to her, like explaining that driving seventeen miles to go to a different grocery store to save $1.70 on apples isn't worth it.

"She says, 'Buzz buzz sting sting run run stupid stupid.'"

"What, no 'oink oink'?" Declan smacks my knee, hard, and gives me a glare that says, *You're ridiculous* and *Stop it* and then his look says *I want to make love right here on the couch in front of your mother.*

And then he kisses me so hard even Mom goes silent.

"So," she interrupts, her voice high and reedy, "we need to get going. Downward Facing Dog is for yoga class, not on my nice Bauhaus sofa."

Declan ignores her and smiles against my mouth. Aha. I'm sensing a trend. He loves to smile while kissing me while defying the people most interested in controlling me. Hmmm. I should think that one through, but the flutter of his fingers against my breast makes me think I'm about to pop my Bauhaus sofa cherry and then my sex starts doing jumping jacks and shouting, *Control me!*

Control me!

"I'm going to class! Need to be there early!" Mom's shaky voice carries through the room at a distance.

Declan's hand leaves my breast and he waves silently, mouth a bit busy. I hear the click of the front door as it shuts and he pulls away, smile intact.

"Mission accomplished."

My face falls. "*That* was your mission? To drive my mom away? I can do that by pretending to be a Republican."

His face becomes a stone mask. "*I'm* a Republican."

I punch his shoulder lightly and laugh. "You almost had me there."

The expression doesn't change.

Oh, hell no. Even Steve was a Democrat. Most of the time.

"What are you?" he asks.

"I'm a Stewartarian."

"You worship *The Daily Show*?"

"It's like my daily mass." My heart is hammering. I hate politics. I don't even really have a party. In Massachusetts almost everyone I know is a Democrat, and if they're not, they're originally from New Hampshire or Maine. So…

"Are you one of those screechy liberals who crams your morals down other people's throats because you view the world through a rigid ideological lens and can't bear to see other people making different choices?" he asks.

"You sound like Rush Limbaugh!" I squeak.

He's laughing, though. "Replace 'liberals' with 'conservatives' and you get the same end." He chuckles quietly, then caresses my face. "I don't care what you believe, as long as I can have a rational conversation with you."

"The only topic where reason goes out the window is cilantro."

"Cilantro?"

"Tastes like soap."

"Same here."

"Oh my God! It's true love!" I clap my hand over my mouth as if that will shove the words back in.

The grin he gives me changes as his eyes shift to something behind me. The clock. "We're going to be late."

Breathe, Shannon. Breathe. Let respiration restart so you don't pass out on top of blurting out that you're in love with him already. It's only been a month. Who falls in love in a month? People on LastShot.com, where you openly confess to having STD lesions, and gamers, that's who.

"And," he says as we stand, stopping me from grabbing a kitchen knife and carving out my vocal cords, "nothing says true love like Mexican food that tastes like laundry detergent."

* * *

One of Mom's friends from college moved in a few towns over and took an old chicken coop on her property and turned it into a yoga studio. Yep—

chicken coop. Except this is like a chicken spa, and if any actual chickens ever set foot in here I think they'd face twenty-five screaming women all searching for their pillow-sized Vera Bradley bags to bash the poor creatures to death.

Declan and I arrive and immediately change the demographics in the room:

1. We lower the average age by a mere two years, but hey, we're outnumbered...

2. Declan alone increases the average income by five figures.

3. He adds a male to the group. The *only* male in the group.

Mom urges us to get in the front row, and I scout it out carefully. Yoga freaks have this *thing* about their space. No one actually, officially, claims a space, but they do in their *minds*, and no matter how much yoga is supposed to be about awareness and acceptance and detachment and flow, so help you bloody GOD if you take a yoga freak's spot in class.

Namaste, motherf—

"I am so glad you're here!" Mom squeals as Declan rolls out his mat. We're barefoot and I can't stop peeking at his feet. For a guy, they're remarkably nice and athletic and groomed. "Metrosexual" is not the word I'd use to describe Declan, but his feet scream *manscaped!* I imagine them sliding up and down my calves...

He starts to stretch and smiles at me, beckoning with his eyes to join him. I bend down to unroll my mat and a popcorn popper goes off.

Wait. That's just my joints.

And twenty old ladies' necks all turning at once when they realize there's a man in the room, and he's not on Viagra.

(At least, I assume he's not. And it's no thanks to me. One inch in the wrong direction with that EpiPen and...)

I shudder and he reaches over to give me an affectionate caress. "You cold?"

Twenty sighs fill the air. Mom appears up front, setting up her blocks and yoga mat. This is Restorative Yoga, which means everyone in the room pays $17 each to lie around on a foam mat and fall asleep. How Mom ever got into this business is still a mystery to me, but anyone who can get paid to make her customers zone out and snore and be *praised wildly* is pretty freaking brilliant as far as I'm concerned.

He leans over for a kiss.

Twenty moans rise up behind us.

And then—scuffling sounds.

"You know Marie will have us do Downward Dog and Cow," someone hisses. A chorus of voices all say "Ooooooh," followed by a whispered frenzy. Those are yoga positions where you shove your butt in the air.

Hold on a second...

"I'll pay your class fee if you give me the spot," says Agnes. I only know her name because the last time I was here all the other women were gossiping about her because allegedly she's a bit of a loose woman. How you label a ninety-year-old woman "loose" is beyond me, but all I can think is *GO AGNES*.

When I'm ninety I hope I'm still doing yoga and that my libido cries out for a piece of a man, Viagra or no Viagra. The clitoris does not have an expiration date. The hard part must be finding a man with similar interests, a similar life timeframe, and one who isn't in a lovely white cardboard box on someone's mantle.

"You think you can always get everything you want, Agnes," one of the other women hisses. "Not everything has a price."

"Some views are priceless," another woman sighs. "I'll pay for two classes if you – "

As I turn to watch the brewing fight behind us, Declan's lips are twitching. He leans over and says, "Ten dollars says Agnes ends up leading a Senior WWF brawl back there."

"MMA is more her style."

"Corrine, I swear!" Agnes shouts. "You can stand there like a mule all you want and refuse to budge, but I know about your bone density levels." Her voice carries an ominous tone.

"You wouldn't!" Corrine cries out. She's seventy-something going on fifty, with a wig from Farrah Fawcett's day. She looks like she's in a wind tunnel. Oh—no. That's just really bad plastic surgery.

"I'll nudge you just enough to fall and you have a hip that's more fragile than Putin's ego."

Wait a minute here. These old ladies are threatening bodily harm and broken bones so they can sit behind my boyfriend and ogle his *ass*?

I crane around behind him and take a good look.

Yep.

Totally worth it.

"Ladies! Ladies!" Declan stands up without using his hands to even touch the ground, displaying ab and core strength that makes everyone freeze, drool, and sigh at once. Someone back there might even have farted.

He holds his hands in the air, palms out, to get the group to pay even more attention to him. "Let's make it a bit more fun, shall we?"

Mom stops her preparations, her finger about to push the button to start the sonorous soundtrack.

"If one of you can guess how Shannon and I met, you can win the—"

Twenty women shriek, "TOILET GIRL!"

"MOM!" I howl.

"Don't shake her hand," Agnes whispers to Corrine, who stares resolutely ahead and doesn't give Agnes a millimeter as my mom comes over to me and Declan with an *Oh, shit* look on her face.

"It's such a charming story!" she says in a stage voice. "My daughter being a professional at the top of her game in business, meeting the billionaire son of James McCormick—"

"The Silver Wolf," Corrine gasps, giving Declan the once-over with eyes like a Terminator robot from one of those movies, evaluating him for specific fleshy characteristics that meet her mission's criteria, which I suspect involve twisting her body against his in non-standard yoga positions. "You look like him."

"My father has a *nickname*?" he mutters, then mumbles quietly to me, "A sexy nickname? Gross."

"Your father is a gorgeous hunk," someone calls out.

"Dad doesn't date anyone over thirty," he says under his breath.

"Oh, goody. My timer doesn't pop for six more years," I hiss.

He flinches, and I can't tell if it's from the radioactive sarcasm in my voice or from the idea of my dating his father. Hopefully, it's both.

This is *not* restorative.

"Ladies! We're running out of time!" Mom calls out, now back in place at her mat. She gives me a fake helpless look and mouths *What can I do?*

More therapy, I mouth.

She gives me a hearty thumbs-up, then leads the class through a series of warmup poses that leave me sweatier than Mom during the height of menopause. Declan hasn't broken a sweat. Six women are trying to share one yoga mat behind him, though.

Soon we're all on our backs, stretched out on the floor, listening to Pink Floyd. If they handed out little LSD stamps before class, this part would be even better. Instead, I hear light snoring, the high-pitched whine of someone's uncalibrated hearing aid, and the sound of Every. Single. Woman getting up at least once during full-body relaxation mode to pee.

The bladder does not acknowledge Restorative Yoga. It's an anarchist when it comes to Savasana pose. *No snooze for you!*

In the dark, "Comfortably Numb" comes on, and I feel something brush against my hip. Declan's hand finds mine and he interlaces our fingers. I relax immediately at his touch, layers of tight muscle giving way, and as his warm palm reminds me that he's there—really there—I wonder if it is true love when you finally find someone else who thinks cilantro tastes like detergent.

His hand, fingers woven into mine like a web, goes slack, too. We're shedding layers through touch, and maybe there's something to this whole Restorative Yoga thing, I think, as a warm cloud of deep bliss surrounds me. Declan shifts his arm so slightly, his palm sliding against mine, and I can feel him smiling.

Sinking deeper, the world fades out and all I am is my hand, touching him, and it's so much more than enough that I dissolve into a state of harmony that slips into a peaceful darkness.

Chapter Ten

"I hope you two die just like that."

Mom's words make my eyes snap open. She's standing over me, the yoga studio's lights on full blaze, and there are about ten other sets of eyes boring down on me.

Us. Me and Declan. I turn my head, confused and fuzzy now as I come out of my slumber, and see he's out cold, still. A big patch of drool covers one side of my mouth and even my hair is a bit soaked at the jaw line.

"You hope we—what?" Instinct tells me to sit up, to run away, to escape from being the focus of the yoga version of Ray Bradbury's *The Crowd*.

"I hope you die just like you are, right now. So cute." All eleven women staring at us like we're part of some modern art exhibit sigh in unison.

Declan's right eyebrow shoots up and he says nothing.

"You want me to *die*?" I ask, incredulous. "In your yoga class?" He squeezes my hand and I try not to laugh.

"No, I mean, you know, in sixty or seventy years. That you two die after a long, happy marriage and plenty of kids and you're peaceful old people who die just like that." Mom's elaboration doesn't help.

"I wanted that, too," Agnes says. "But my husband, Jerry, had other plans."

"How did he die?" Mom asks. But she asks as if she knows the answer already.

Agnes looks at me. "He got his hand stuck in a toilet and couldn't get out. I was on a tour of Niagara Falls with my church group for three days and he starved to death."

Declan groans, his body curling in a bit. He's trying not to laugh, and he shakes, abs rippling against his tight Lycra shirt, his ass tightening.

"Ooooh, keep it up. Nice glutes," someone says. That just makes him laugh harder. Now I sit up and let go of his hand. For some reason, I'm jealous—jealous!—and don't like all these people eyeing my man candy.

He's mine.

"Your husband didn't really die like that, did he?" I'm cynical enough to think there's no way that story is true, but just gullible enough to worry that if I assume it's a joke, and it isn't, that I'll destroy an old woman's feelings.

"No. He died porking a retail clerk at the mall. They were on the elevator. He was a security guard. Heart attack. The man didn't touch me for seven years and then he goes and sticks it to the pretzel stand girl."

That makes me bark with laughter as Mom waves her hands behind Agnes and mouths *It's true*.

Oh, hell. I can't win.

"I hope I die in the arms of someone I love," Mom announces. Declan's laughter comes to an abrupt halt, the change so distinct it makes the hair on my arms prickle. Something in Mom's declaration hit a nerve with him, and it makes me see how little I really know about him.

He stands, fluid and graceful, then yawns. This is no normal yawn, though. It's a lion's roar, with arms stretched nice and high, his belly button exposed as he reaches for the sky, stretching and extending his muscles and joints. The body on display for us all is, decidedly, the nicest eye candy ever. Fine, Swiss eye candy. Candy made from slave-free, ninety-percent cacao farmed by happy rural cooperative workers working to save the whales.

"Can I just touch him, once?" someone asks. "It's like all those Nike ads with the sweaty, hot men come to life, within reach. I thought they were all done with trick photography. This—this is like learning Bigfoot is real."

A green wave of mist covers my vision. What is wrong with me? I'm jealous of women who haven't needed to use birth control since the moon landing.

But yes—I am.

"Bigfoot is real, Irene," Agnes says to the owner of the disembodied voice. "I saw it on the Discovery Channel last week."

"You're so naïve, Agnes. That show is just trick photography and some guy with too much hair on his body. My Dave was that way. The man could go around the house without a shirt on and you swore he was wearing a mohair sweater. That's all Bigfoot is."

The two descend into bickering as Mom shoos the crowd out, thanking them for coming and talking about seeing them next week.

Declan snuggles up to me. "You like what you see?"

"Mmmm, eye candy. Zero calories and better than licking a lollipop."

"I've got a lollipop you can lick."

Mom, of course, happens to walk over to us just as he says that, and she pretends to be shocked, then pretends she heard nothing.

"So, Declan, did Shannon invite you over for Easter dinner?"

Huh? We never discussed this. Why is Mom acting like I—

"No, Marie, she didn't," he says slowly, not making eye contact with either of us, his body bent in half as he rolls up his yoga mat. We're greeted with the mighty fine view of his ass, and we sigh in unison.

I elbow Mom—hard.

"I can't help it!" she hisses.

"You better help it. It's icky."

"You're right! You're right." She appears to take me seriously. "It is icky. I'll stop right now." She gives me a look that's genuinely contrite.

"Well," Mom says loudly as Declan turns and faces us, "even if Shannon didn't invite you, I'm inviting you."

His eyes travel slowly from my face to Mom's. "When is Easter?" he finally asks.

"This Sunday!" she sputters. "In three days." With a frown, she says, "But I'm sure you have plans with your family."

"We haven't celebrated Easter in more than ten years," he says in a matter-of-fact tone.

"How awful!" Mom exclaims, grabbing his arm. Her eyes almost glisten with tears, and she's truly shocked. She pauses. "Are you Jewish? Is that why?"

"No."

The lack of additional information unsettles both me and Mom. Declan has this way of being shut off. He's not cold, exactly. It's more like talking with a lawyer who isn't going to give one single additional bit of information than is necessary in court.

Except we're not in the middle of a legal proceeding. We're in my mother's yoga studio, talking about a holiday where the Easter bunny and a giant ham prevail. What's up with him?

"Mom, if he were Jewish he wouldn't have celebrated before. He just said it's been more than ten years since…" I turn to him. "Since your mom died?"

He nods. But nothing more. He's so…wound, suddenly.

"Will you be there?" Mom asks, her smile so sweet and warm. "We have a loud, crazy family and I'm the queen of it all. And I make a killer ham."

"You buy it from the ham place down the street," I say. "The kind with the crusted sugar on the edge, all spiral sliced, and then she makes the sweet potatoes with little marshmallows..." My stomach growls.

He thaws. "Who can pass that up?" Eyes that were green tundra seconds ago warm up, and his body loosens. "Thank you, Marie. What time?"

"Two for dinner, and at three we do the Easter egg hunt." Mom looks happier than Martha Stewart being told that Gordon Ramsay's coming for dinner.

"What can I bring?"

"Your helicopter." She is practically jumping out of her skin with excitement.

"Um, I was thinking more like a bottle of wine, Marie." Declan wraps his arm around my waist and presses an absent-minded kiss against my temple. He smells like sweat and comfort, spices and safety.

"Okay, fine. The helicopter would be one hell of an entrance." She just doesn't know when to stop.

"Where would he land it, Mom? In Dad's garden?"

"Why not? He hasn't planted anything in there this season yet."

"How about I arrive in my own SUV, wearing something other than a suit, and I bring suitable Easter egg hunt items and a bottle of wine?"

"And your Batman costume," I add with a smirk at Mom.

"Leave our sex life out of this," he stage whispers.

Mom turns pink and stammers. "I—I'm so glad you'll be there!" She skitters off to the office.

I hit Declan in the pec. My fingers crack. "Why did you say that?"

"Because I like to beat her at her own game." His smile is so impish I stand on tiptoes and give him a grateful kiss.

"You'll never win," I say, sighing.

"Never say never."

* * *

"You need to pee," Tyler says as Declan walks in the front door of my parents' house on Easter afternoon. It's two o'clock and my boyfriend (that still gives me shivers to say it) is punctual. And, as promised, he drove his SUV, is wearing a long-sleeved, blue button-down with the sleeves rolled up to the elbows and jeans that fit him achingly well, and holds a lovely bottle of wine.

Declan bends down to be at eye level with my four-year-old nephew, who has his standard, serious look on his face. Little bow-tie lips, short brown hair, and brown eyes fringed by eyelashes so long they reach the ceiling.

"Thanks, buddy, but I don't need to pee."

"You need to pee!" Tyler insists as Carol comes running from the kitchen and whisks him away to the bathroom.

I get a questioning look from Declan and try to explain. "Potty training. And Tyler has a language disorder, so right now he confuses 'you' and 'I.'"

The lights go on for Declan. "I see. So he was saying '*I* need to pee.'" He laughs. "I hope he made it."

Carol starts clapping and cheering from afar.

"I'll take that as a yes." Declan's kiss is polite and brief, so routine it warms my heart. That is the kind of kiss you give someone you're becoming very comfortable with, and I love it.

Love him.

"Declan! You're here!" Mom comes barreling out of the kitchen wearing a red apron that says "Will Cook for Sex." She gives him a warm, motherly hug. He's a head taller than her and yet she's the one enveloping him. He closes his eyes and surrenders to the embrace. A tiny corner of my heart grows a little more.

"Wine, as promised," he tells her, handing off a bottle of something white. Looking artfully around the empty front room, he says with some care in a whisper, "And I have a bunch of plastic eggs stuffed with candy and toys out in my car. Where should I put them?"

Mom's grin splits her happy face and she gives him a big kiss on the cheek. "You sweetie! When we're ready for the egg hunt we'll just grab them and hide them." She holds the bottle away from her, squinting to read the label. "Jason! Come see Declan and take this chilled bottle out of here!"

Dad walks down the hall and joins us. He's wearing a matching apron, khakis, and no shoes or socks. I think Dad is allergic to socks and shoes.

"Declan!" They shake hands enthusiastically.

"Good to see you." Mom hands Dad the bottle.

"White!" she chirps.

"Thank you," Dad says to Declan. "Want a beer?"

"What about the wine, Jason?" Mom screeches, scandalized.

Declan and Dad ignore her, like they planned it in advance. Dad shoots me a wink.

"Sure. Whatcha got?"

"You like stouts? I've got some microbrew from this little place in Framingham..." Declan walks away, following Dad, and just like that, he's integrated into the household.

I stand in my own childhood home and look around the living room. Everyone's congregated in the tiny kitchen and I overhear Amy telling Carol about running in the marathon. Mom and Dad could buy a five-thousand-square-foot mansion in Osterville with an enormous living room and everyone would still cram into the kitchen to talk and taste and hang out.

Declan breezed into the house, was told he needed to pee by a child, offered up a bottle of wine, and boom! Dad takes him to his Man Cave in the backyard like we're married and have been together forever.

I'm sensing a trend here.

This might actually happen. Me and Declan.

Carol walks into the living room, rubbing vanilla-scented lotion on her hands. She stares at me for a second, eyebrows raised. "You okay?"

"Dad just took Declan to the Man Cave."

"He's being accepted into the tribe."

"Is that good or bad?" I give her a helpless look and sink down onto the couch. The springs are shot, so I literally sink down, my feet flying off the floor. I bury my head in my hands.

Carol stands over me and finishes rubbing the lotion. "I think you're afraid of success."

"What? No. No, I'm not. I never had a problem with Dad taking Steve into the Land of Grunts and Farts." Dad has a little hundred-square-foot shed that he winterized a while ago. It's got a television, ancient lounge chairs Mom tried to throw away years ago, and all his old sci-fi paperbacks he's been collecting since the 1960s, lined on homemade shelves.

He illegally piped a wood stove in there, and has an old milk jug I suspect doubles as a toilet in a pinch. Sometimes he and Mom have fights so intense he sleeps out there. Just for one night, though. The Man Cave smells like male sweat, Old Spice, and onions. Seriously. There's a minor methane crisis in there. Jeffrey says it smells like Grandpa.

"Dad only took him back there to be nice to you. He hated Steve."

"I know." Once Steve dumped me they *allllll* came out of the woodwork to tell me what an ass Steve was, and Dad led the charge. He was like pressure cooker. Once you popped the seal on the lid, more steam than you knew existed came pouring out.

Enough to burn if you weren't careful.

116

"'Pearls after swine' was the exact phrase he used all the time," she adds.

"He said that about you and Todd, too."

"I know."

"No, like, at your wedding. And when Jeffrey was born. And then Tyler, and—"

"Got it. Don't need my nose rubbed in it."

Silence hangs between us for a second. I look like a hybrid of Mom and Dad. Carol, though, looks most like Mom. Lighter blonde hair, blue eyes, a round face with dimples, and plump cheeks that make her look perennially cheerful, even when she's not smiling. She's the oldest, and life hasn't been easy these past few years.

"Any luck with jobs?" I ask. She's the one who got me into mystery shopping. Back when I was hired on full-time she had a great full-time job. Then Tyler began having huge behavioral problems, Todd dropped off the face of the earth, and she was laid off. Mom and Dad have helped. Carol mystery shops with the kids when she can, and she's living on unemployment and some vague government assistance I don't quite understand. She has a degree, and loads of determination, but not a lot of time or hope.

"I have an interview with a call center. Night shift. Mom says she and Dad can help with babysitting." Defeat oozes in her voice.

"Minimum wage?"

"No, actually. More like a standard three-to-eleven shift. I'd have to rely on Mom and Dad too much. it's not fair to them."

"They love Jeffrey and Tyler," I protest.

"I know. It's just...you don't have kids. You don't understand." Her eyes shift down and she looks like a very serious, contemplative version of our mother. The dissonance is hard to reconcile. I don't think I've ever seen Mom look...reflective.

"No, you're right. I don't." I do want kids someday. Watching Carol struggle the way she has definitely made me extend "someday" by a few years, though. Tyler and Jeffrey are the best kids ever (I'm biased), but they haven't been easy to raise without help.

"And you're dating a hot billionaire."

I roll my eyes and she smirks. Ah. Now she looks like Mom again.

Hot Billionaire chooses that moment to walk in, overhearing Carol's comment "You're dating another guy named Hot Billionaire?" His easy touch as he wraps an arm around my waist just adds to her embarrassment. I remember when she brought Todd home, when I was thirteen, and I thought he was so hot. Jealousy poured through me then, as Todd would give her hugs and kisses and little love pats. *That* was love, I thought. Back then, before Todd turned out to be pond scum.

Declan's not Todd.

Carol turns bright pink. It looks like she poured a bottle of Pepto-Bismol all over her face. "We thought you were in the Man Cave, grunting and eating roast meat off a stick," she says.

"We were, until the little boys found us, and now your dad is playing horsey with them and he

118

sent me in here for a rescue team."

Carol laughs and takes the chance to escape. "I'll rescue him!"

"Dinner's soon! Declan, can you help set the table?" Mom comes out of the kitchen, her hair so thoroughly sprayed and set in stone by some chemical that will likely be proven in ten years to cause cancer, but by God keeps her hair in place even as she cooks.

"Sure." He winks at me and walks toward Mom. "Where's the dining room?"

Mom leads him through the kitchen into the formal dining room, the sanctuary of Good Food and the room we use exactly three times a year: Easter, Thanksgiving, and Christmas. When not in use for a holiday, the dining table doubles as a storage facility for junk mail, LEGO toys Mom finds while vacuuming, and random light bulbs Dad needs to remember to replace with LEDs but never does.

Mom's really pulled out all the stops, with a pale blue linen tablecloth and matching napkins. I wonder which thrift store she got that deal from, and then I see the glasses. Matching crystal glasses at each seat, the tops edged with gold.

"Like my table?" she asks proudly.

"Where'd you get it all?" I ask, definitely admiring. Mom and I have a shared love for "thrifting" and yard-saling.

"Savers!" she exclaims, then catches Declan's confused look.

"What's Savers?"

Amy happened to come into the room and is halfway to greeting me and Declan, arms stretched out for a hug, when she stops cold at Declan's words. "You don't know what Savers is?"

"Get me some smelling salts," Mom jokes, "because I'm about to faint. Declan, we have to take you thrifting!"

"Thrifting?" He seems amused.

"Shopping at thrift shops. Yard sales. Estate sales. That sort of thing. And Savers is a chain of thrift shops."

"Used items?" He still seems confused. "So you only buy used items? Like antiques?"

Mom's turn to look confused. "Declan, you've never bought something used?"

"An antique. Sure. Dad buys them all the time for the office and his house. But otherwise...no."

"You just shop in regular stores for everything?"

"I have shoppers who do that for me. Unless it's clothing. Then I just go to a tailor."

"Oh," Mom says quietly. An awkward pause fills the air.

"I would love to go 'thrifting' with you, Marie," he says with a smile. "It sounds like fun."

He is officially the Best Billionaire Boyfriend I have ever had.

Mom relaxes and points to the fridge. "Can you get the butter lamb, Declan? It's time to get the food on the table."

His face goes slack, the friendliness replaced by a kind of tempered shock he's obviously trying to hide. "Butter lamb?"

I laugh, trying to get him to chill out. "A few generations back, Dad's family was from the Buffalo area. Polish. There's this tradition where you—"

"Where you have a pound of butter that's pressed and formed into the shape of a lamb, and you put it out on the table at Easter," he says.

Everyone freezes. Jaws drop. Eyes open wide.

"You know about the butter lamb?"

His hands are shaking, just a tad, as he shoves them in the front pockets of his jeans. "Um, sure. My mom was from that area. We had one every year." He swallows so hard we can all hear the click in his throat, and his face is uncertain, eyes blinking rapidly. "I haven't seen once since…"

"Since she died?" I ask gently, my hand reaching out to his forearm for reassurance. He doesn't move, doesn't flinch, doesn't change his stance. I want to ask him again how his mother died, but this really isn't the time.

Nod.

"Then wonderful!" Mom gushes. "Not wonderful that your mother died, but wonderful that you can reconnect with an old family tradition." She reaches for his shoulders and directs him to the fridge, then walks past him to the stove to stir something. A timer goes off and she mutters to herself.

Declan sets the yellow lamb on the table and looks out the back sliding doors toward the yard, where Dad is pushing Tyler on the swing set.

"Can we go outside?" he asks in a ragged voice.

"Of course." We head toward the door and I pause with my hand on it. "If this is too much, we can leave. Go somewhere quiet and—"

He takes both my hands in his and smiles at me with troubled eyes. "It's more than enough, but not too much. I want to stay. Your family is lovely."

"My family is crazy."

"Crazy can be lovely."

Chapter Eleven

By the time dinner and the Easter egg hunt are over, everyone has turned into a human potato bug, round and grey, a series of roly-polies stuffed silly. Conversation has devolved into exclamations of how good all the food was and groans about how our stomachs are about to explode.

"Can I see your childhood bedroom?" Declan asks. He's relaxed considerably since he first arrived.

"Want to examine my Barbies?" But I stand and reach out for his hand, leading him up the stairs. Jeffrey and Tyler are in the backyard shrieking and chasing Amy with little toy guns, shooting foam bullets at her. They miss every single time.

Dad has actually undone his belt and the top button of his khakis, and rests in a lounge chair like Al Bundy, one hand tucked in his waistband.

Mom's in the kitchen fussing over the leftovers. There's enough food to feed an army.

"My room isn't anything special," I explain as we walk up the carpeted stairs. When Amy turned sixteen Mom finally got her wish—cream carpet—and even now, more than five years later, it feels weird to me. I went away to college and the house had industrial green, flat carpet and came home to a *Better Homes and Gardens* spread.

"It's special because it's yours."

We're greeted, first, by the giant head of Justin Bieber on my bedroom door.

"Nice. You were a Belieber?"

"That's a sick, sick joke from Amy."

I open the door and Justin steps aside. "Voilà!" I sweep my arm around the room. White furniture, all of it "thrifted" and refinished by Dad. Simple sheer curtains. An entire wall of cork squares with push-pinned articles and pictures from teen magazines. A ton of shells from vacations to Cape Cod.

Nothing amazing. The amazing part, actually, is that Mom hasn't made me clear it out yet. She claimed Carol's old bedroom as a yoga studio a few years ago. My time is likely ticking.

Declan's hands are all over me suddenly, his lips on my shoulder, caresses in places that tell me exactly what he's thinking, and he's not thinking about Justin Bieber.

At least, I hope not.

"We can't have sex in here!" I hiss. Jeffrey and Tyler are thumping up and down the carpeted stairs now, with Jeffrey calling out numbers. An impromptu game of Hide and Go Seek is afoot, and I don't want the kids to catch us hiding something of Declan inside Auntie Shannon.

"Why not?"

"For one, my twin bed is so small you'll poke

my eye out before you hit the target—"

"Is *this* the target?"

I struggle to speak as electric jolts shoot through me like I'm mainlining a battery. The heat pouring out of his rock-solid chest and hips that press into my own belly makes my knees go weak. Teenage Shannon who spent many fitful nights dreaming about this moment is clashing with Responsible Shannon.

"And for two, I don't want anyone in my family to hear!"

As if on cue, Jeffrey shouts, "Ready or not, here I come!"

"I want to hear *you* say that," Declan whispers as he bites my earlobe.

"You—I—what are you—oh my God," I gasp as he slips his hands under my waistband and does unspeakable things.

"Then let's go have sex in your car."

"We can't have sex in my *car*!" Teenage Shannon is, like, totally grossed out by the idea of finally having sex in her parents' house but doing it in a car that looks like it should be sprayed down by the mosquito truck is even worse. All the Shannons agree on this point, even the pulsing little Shannon in my pants, the one that keeps screaming *Yes yes yes* even though she doesn't have a mouth.

"Why not? We already had sex in mine, so fair is fair. Your turn."

"I drive a car with a *dead insect* on top of it."

"Maybe that's my real fetish."

"Oh, toilets aren't enough?"

"I'll show you a fetish or two."

A rush of warm electricity fires out from my core through every single pore on my body, and I'm about to agree to whatever he wants and throw in a few of my own requests as well, when—

"SHANNON!" Dad's voice is joyful and blessedly ingenuous. "Let's get ready for ice cream."

"Ice cream?" Declan murmurs, fingers sliding up to find my throbbing point that makes me inhale so sharply a strand of hair gets caught in my nostril.

"It's trad"—my voice hitches with arousal and groaning need—"ition. We stuff ourselves silly and then go out for chocolate-dipped cones. The local ice cream joint opens today. Then we go to the movies."

"Ice cream and the movies on Easter? I love your family."

"I love your fingers."

"I have other long bits of me you might love, too."

"THANNON AND DECLAN!" Jeffrey screams, right outside my door. Oh, no. Did I lock it? Did Declan? "It ith time for eyth cream!"

"I love eyth cream," Declan says as he kisses me, his tongue probing deep, wet, and luscious. This is the kind of kiss a man gives a woman when there are no preliminaries, where you go right for the marrow and the soul, because all those surface layers peel away with a single touch.

The kind of kiss you can enjoy and treasure for the rest of your life without ever experiencing any other kind.

"Hey, Shannon, are you guys—" Amy barges through the door the same way she did when we were kids and living at home. Hell, the same way she does in our shared apartment *now*.

Declan smiles against my lips, pulling his hands out of my pants, leaving me frantic and disassembled.

"Oh, you two are having a different kind of dessert," she mumbles, pulling back and closing the door, but not quite fast enough.

"Auntie Thannon! Declan! Eyth cream time!" Jeffrey bursts into the room and slides between us, wrapping his little arms around my waist. "Group hug!"

Amy snickers.

"Group hug?" Declan ruffles his hair anyhow, but the disappointment and skepticism in his voice makes me snicker, too.

"Ice cream and the newest Pixar movie will have to be a poor substitute."

A spreading grin lights up his face. "No. A great substitute."

I smack his shoulder. "Hey!"

"We have all the time in the world," he adds, pressing a kiss against my cheek.

"Groth," Jeffrey mutters, pulling on my hand. "Eyth cream!"

"You owe me a double, kid," I say as we all head downstairs to the waiting crew.

Chapter Twelve

"You are the worst wife *ever*," I hiss to Amanda as we get out of the Turdmobile. We've parked a few blocks away from the credit union and she's nattering on about strategy in between grilling me about my relationship with Declan. A quick glance at my car and the light bounces off a bunch of little sparkly things littering my floor. The Easter Bunny was good to Jeffrey and Tyler. A little too good. Plus, Mom still insists on giving her own kids a basket, so I have enough chocolate egg foil wrappers on the floor of my car to build three disco balls.

I kill the engine and climb out of the car. A kid on a skateboard who looks like he's about twelve, with a Justin Bieber haircut and a Minecraft t-shirt, waves as he skates past and says, "Your car's a piece of shit." His laughter trails off.

So does my self-confidence.

"Ignore him. Focus on me. Tell me every detail about Declan. Your bedroom after Easter dinner?" We have both been so busy for the past two weeks. Amanda was at a big mystery shopper's convention in Kansas City last week, and this is the first chance we've had to talk in person. It figures: I live a dull, boring life for freaking *ever*, and just when it gets good she's not around. And now we can catch up, but we're about to pretend to be married.

While I describe my sex life.

Hmmm.

"No – Jeffrey stopped us."

She frowns. "Did you seriously have sex in a limo, on a helicopter, and in a lighthouse?"

"Yes."

"You can do it in a car. You can do it in a bar. You can do it with long hair. You can do it in the air. You can do it in a limo, you can do it—you're a bimbo!"

"Hey!"

"You can do it in a lighthouse. You can…" Her voice trails off. "What rhymes with lighthouse?"

"Winehouse?"

She shudders, then laughs. "Day-um!" She stretches the word out like it's taffy. "Declan has the refractory period of a seventeen-year-old if you had that much sex in one night."

I blush.

"In a *helicopter*?" she squeaks. Squinting, she rolls her eyes up, as if trying to imagine it. "How did you not fall out a door or something?"

"It was, um…one-sided." My face is as red as her painted lips.

"A one-sided helicopter?"

"A one-sided sex act. On the way home."

"You gave him a—oh. Got it." She gives me a high-five. I smack her palm back and feel a roiling sense of doom in my gut. Are we seriously talking about all the ways I had sex with a man—a very, very attractive man—while walking to a mystery shop in which we have to pretend to be married?

"So…I am guessing you didn't go back to that Mexican joint to collect Steve. "

I snort. "No. Though Declan was shocked when Mom gave him a big old stuffed bunny and his own basket that contained half of the Walgreen's candy aisle."

She nudges me. "It's getting serious if Marie's making Declan a basket."

"And you'll be proud to know I deleted Steve's eleventy billion texts. He's such an ass. Why did I ever date him?" Between her comment about Declan and Mom and my own feeling of detachment about Steve, I think I might be moving on. Finally.

She uses her hands to make it clear she agrees. "We've all been asking that question for years!"

"All?"

"Me. Josh. Greg. Amy. Your dad. Hell, even Chuckles would agree if he could talk."

"Chuckles is an equal-opportunity hater, so his contempt for Steve isn't surprising."

"He was on Twitter and Facebook chasing you down. It was pathetic."

"Chuckles?"

She makes a face. "Steve."

I saw the tags and tweets briefly before he deleted them. I'm guessing someone got to him and convinced him that starting hashtags like

#freeShannon and #billionaireaggression wasn't exactly good for his business prospects. I'm too aglow with the newly emerging relationship with Declan, from yoga to butter lambs, to care.

"I know." The air is crisp and clean after a morning downpour. A cold front came in and swept out a bunch of oppressive humidity, leaving this spring day for sunshine and that damp-around-the-edges kind of world that feels like its just been baptized.

"You really like Declan." Amanda pauses and looks closely at me. My heart soars and sinks at the same time. She's looking *at* me. Not through me. Open-minded and non-judgmental, my bestie is trying to tell me something.

"I do." How can I explain how much he affects me, the longing inside even when I just saw him twelve hours ago at Easter? The sour taste of Steve's "date" with me is washed away by the rain. Whatever bitterness I've been clinging to has dissipated these last few weeks. Steve is a non-entity in my life now. He let me loose.

I should thank him, in fact, because I would never have broken up with him, and if he hadn't set me free I would never have met Declan. Never have succumbed to this attractive man. Never made love in a limo or basked in the afterglow in a lighthouse on the harbor. Never had Declan over for Easter, or had second dessert at his apartment long after the kids' movie ended…

Never been Toilet Girl.

She squeezes my shoulder. "I'm really happy

for you." Amanda pauses, then mumbles, "Would a lesbian wear this shade of lavender?" Her hair is still black, lips bright red, and she's wearing a conservative suit. It makes her look like something out of a 1980s music video. Her question throws me out of my thoughts.

"Would you stop asking me what lesbians do?" I throw my hands in the air and lower my voice as passersby start to stare. "How would I know?"

She seems chastened. "Fine. I just don't want to blow our cover."

"We're pretending to be two women married to each other so we can apply for a mortgage using joint income. I don't think Greg could find a more boring mystery shop if he tried." The shop requirements were clear. The day after I came out of the hospital last week, Amanda and Josh had gone to a different branch of the credit union and posed as a married heterosexual couple. They were treated according to the institution's protocol. Now the question is: will the bank officers treat a gay couple differently?

"Remember the vacuum cleaner secret shops?" she says in a voice laced with indignation.

I flinch. "Okay...so he could find something more boring." Thirty minutes with a canister vacuum cleaner salesman demonstrating dual-level suckage action had the potential to be nice and porny, but instead it was like bad sex.

You just want to grab your things and get out of there as fast as possible and avoid having your feet sucked on.

My phone buzzes. "Let me guess," Amanda says, closing her eyes and touching her head with her envelope, like some old talk show skit. "It's Steve."

I check. She's right.

We should do dinner again. Without being rudely interrupted, he texts.

Okay, I write back, then indulge in a giant wave of self-loathing. Why did I say "okay"?What else should I say? This is the umpteenth text from him about that night in the Mexican place. Declan's timely appearance and deliciously engaging pseudo-kidnapping makes my toes tingle right now, my body on fire with the memory. Like a cat in a hot spot of sunshine, all I want to do is stretch and purr.

Steve makes me want to hiss and claw something. And yet I still say "okay" when he doesn't get the hint. Maybe my idea of a hint isn't strong enough.

I haven't told Amanda everything about Declan. How he seemed jealous, so possessive, coming straight from New Zealand and tracking me down, taking me by limo to his helicopter, then riding around the city until we landed on the island. How he was so charming and controlled at Mom's yoga. The way he emotionally disarms her, but without being rude. The way he makes me feel so secure in just being true to myself.

I slow my pace a bit, wondering if I'm walking funny. I should be. More tingles. I share everything with her, so this is new. Keeping it all to myself makes it have more meaning. Savoring what Declan and I have, and our combined desire to have so much more of it going forward, isn't so much a secret as it is private.

Personal.

Ours.

Mine and Declan's, something we share with no one else. I want to hang on to that for just a little longer, before Mom starts booking reception halls and ordering roses dipped in dye that matches some obscure bra strap Kate Middleton wore at her third polo game with the future king.

"Why are you seeing Steve at all?" Amanda asks.

"Masochism." It's an old joke, but that doesn't mean it's not true.

She speeds up until we're walking at a fast clip and almost at the main door to the credit union. The building looks like every other brick business building with white trim, and a discreet white sign with the name is centered above a bank of glass doors. Warnings dot the entrance:

Remove all sunglasses, hats and hoods. You are being recorded.

Sometimes I think about flashing my boobies for the poor schmuck whose job it is to sit in front of a bank of security cameras and keep an eye out for danger. A little light in a dreary job, you know? I made the mistake of saying this to Mom once. She did it.

Turns out my cousin Vito is a mall cop and was nearly blinded by the sight of Aunt Marie's tatas. He still calls her Aunt Antiviagra. She thinks he's speaking an Italian endearment.

"Don't flash the cameras," Amanda hisses as we walk in. She really does know me too well.

"I won't."

Grabbing my arm, Amanda pauses in the foyer. "You okay?" The way she peers intently into my eyes makes me realize she's really asking whether I've recovered from the bee stings. From the enormity of everything with Declan.

"Yes."

"You came back to work kind of fast."

"I needed to. You ever been bed-ridden with my mom taking care of you?"

"I thought Declan came by every day!"

"He did." I smile at the thought. Mom was practically feeding me chewed-up food from her own mouth and giving me water from an eyedropper. That whole "Oh, my poor baby almost died" stuff required a rescuer. Declan had fit the bill. Except for his time in New Zealand on that business trip, he'd been by my side each day.

And then he'd swooped in on my dinner with Steve and taught me how much fun helicopters can be. I shiver with the memory.

"True love means having your boyfriend watch the *The Sapphires* and *The Heat* three nights in a row with you," Amanda says with a sigh.

True love means being made love to above the city lights, I think, but of course I can't say that. Or in his apartment, which smells like fine cologne, pine, and a special soap. Someone in a suit steps through the doors and ignores us. Then I realize what Amanda just said.

"What boyfriend?" I ask.

She looks confused. "Declan. What other boyfriend do you have other than that electronic bedside-table monstrosity you call Edward Cullen?" Her face scrunches up. "And it's about as old as him, too."

I grab her hand and lace my fingers through hers. "You're the only boyfriend I need, sweetie." Standing on tiptoes, I kiss her cheek.

She jumps back like I've poked her with a cattle prodder. "Greg better give us a bonus for this one."

"He has to come with Josh and do the male-male shop, so I don't think there will be any bonuses."

"Poor Josh. They'll look like a bear and a twink."

My turn to jump like I've been electro-shocked. "Huh? What's that mean?"

The receptionist is giving us nervous looks. Amanda nudges me. "Never mind. You really don't watch enough cable television."

"What does that have to do with—"

She puts her arm around me and pushes us both through the main door into the cool, marble-floored bank, the scent of money filling the air. "Let's get this done and over with."

"I agree. I can't be married to you longer than one hour."

Within ten minutes we're ushered into a glass-walled room with no real door, filled with dark oak furniture, brightly patterned carpeting floors, and a no-nonsense balding man who looks like he eats entire rolls of antacids for fun.

Jim Purlman is the senior mortgage officer for the credit union and asks us how we met.

Amanda and I exchange confused looks. "You mean, like, how we were in the same class in third grade?" she blurts out.

Jim looks like he's half Irish and half something else, with a beet-red nose and eyebrows that haven't been tamed since 1977. The skin under his eyes is paper thin and baggy, and what hair he has is grey, grown in a combover style I haven't seen anywhere other than in old square photographs from the 1960s in my mom's photo albums. The physical kind that smell like old cigarette smoke and liver spot cream.

But he breaks out into a kind grin and says, "What a wonderful love story. Sweethearts since you were little. Found your soul mate young. You two have kids?" He leans his forearms against the glass-topped desk and waits in anticipation for our answer.

I'm struck mute. We'd been told this set of evaluations came at the request of the credit union's board, a reaction to complaints. Jim's response is absolutely not what we were expecting.

Amanda saves the day, reaching for my hand and stroking my wrist with her thumb. A tingling shoots through my body, and it's not the last remnants of the EpiPen's contents. Her eyes meet mine and holy smokes, ladies and gentlemen, we have some acting.

At least, I hope it's acting. Because I am completely into Declan.

"Fate brought us together on the playground and we're hoping it will be kind to us in the kids department." She smiles so sweetly at me that my pulse races and my cheeks flush. There's a settled passion in the way she carries herself, and Jim hunches slightly in his chair, as if relaxing from approval.

"I'm sure you'll find the right man—" He shakes his head slightly. "Er, sorry. The right *path* to have the family you deserve."

Amanda lets go of my hand and puts hers on my knee. Thoughts of Declan set my core on fire. Being touched at all like this, in a partner kind of way, seems to set my screwy wiring into ablaze mode.

"You look like you're about to cry," Jim says.

I reach up and wipe a watery eye. "We're still overjoyed we were allowed to be married," I answer.

"When was that?"

"Two weeks ago, at our town's courthouse."

"So you have a marriage certificate?" he asks.

"Do you need to see it?" To Jim, Amanda's shift in personality can't be noticed, but I get what she's doing now. Legally married heterosexual couples don't need to show a marriage certificate to apply for joint income mortgages, so if he asks, we must note it on the evaluation.

"Oh, no!" he exclaims. "I just meant it must be

great to know you can be married and have all those legal protections."

And just then, someone taps on the glass. I turn toward the sound and my entire body goes cold, frozen like a popsicle.

Standing before me is Monica Raleigh.

Steve's *mother*.

"Shannon!" she exclaims. Thankfully, I've used my real first name on the application here for the mystery shop. But I absolutely cannot break my disguise, and therefore Monica can't know we're here on an evaluation. Absolutely not. No failed shop for this one.

Even if it kills me.

Chapter Thirteen

I stand on shaky legs and she gives me a half-hug, the kind where you can't tell whether the other person has a pulse or not. A cloud of Cinnabar perfume fills my nose and the back of my throat, the taste like rancid cinnamon.

"I haven't seen you in so long," she adds. It's been a year, yes. But Monica never liked me. Ever. Not one bit. Her fakery should be lauded, because she put on a surface act about me. Doing the bare minimum was her form of liking me. A familiar, low-grade shaking begins inside my body, as if my bones were starting to rattle from the first signs of an earthquake.

She looks like a shrunken version of Steve, with the same slightly negative set to her jaw, as if the world has to prove that any shred of positivity is possible. Her default is suspicion and pessimism.

I used to think that was a sign of intelligence, as if being pessimistic meant you just had figured out The Truth long before everyone else did. Now I think it's just a nice cover for being a bit of an asshole and not knowing how to find your way out.

She looks like Steve, except she's a bird. All that's missing are wings. Her waist is thicker than her breast, her legs are scrawny, her feet splay out, and her resemblance to a bird wouldn't be so sharply distinctive if she didn't henpeck everyone.

She also has eyebrows that lift perpetually, making me think she's questioning everything I say.

"Amelia!" she exclaims as she turns to Amanda, who leaps up and practically curtseys. Monica does that to some people. She has the air of a queen and the snootiness of a social climber. Steve and I dated for *how* many years and the woman doesn't remember my best friend's name?

Amanda doesn't correct her. It would be like trying to correct King Joffrey. You'd be beheaded in seconds.

"What are you two doing here?" she asks.

"Hello, Monica," Jim says, standing and coming around the desk. He looks like he's part wolf, predator eyes devouring her. Monica's wearing something stylish from one of the boutiques near Neiman Marcus in the Natick Mall —oh, excuse me, the Natick *Collection*. Can't call it a mall. Every other town calls their enclosed shopping center a mall, but Natick's developers appear to wish they were designing Rodeo Drive.

And Monica acts like she lives on it, even though she's really a suburban mom.

"Why, Jim!" she exclaims, like Scarlett O'Hara in *Gone With the Wind*. I half expect to hear *fiddle-dee-dee* come out of her mouth and for South Boston to burst into flames. Have the Red Sox lose in the seventh game of the World Series and that might actually happen.

"Amanda and Shannon are here to apply for a mortgage," Jim explains.

Amanda and I share a look of horror and professionalism, tenuously balanced at the half-and-half point.

"A mortgage? You're buying property?" Monica's eyes light up. "How ambitious of you, Shannon. I thought you'd stay in that dead-end job forever and never show any chutzpah. Steve taught you some good skills, didn't he? I'm sure you appreciate everything he did for you all those years."

Screech. Stop the merry-go-round, because someone needs to get knocked off her high horse.

I can't let Jim know that I used to date Steve. Not, at least, until Amanda and I finish this evaluation from hell. I know I'm in hell because Monica is the queen here. She could marry Hades and have him whipped in no time.

Amanda's all too aware of the predicament, but can also see smoke coming out of my ears, so she steps between me and Monica, opening her mouth, just as Jim says:

"The newlyweds are here to buy their first house together. Isn't that something?"

You date a guy for a few years and you get to know his mother fairly well, even if she has a stick up her butt so long she could pick oranges with it. Monica won't leave now because she's a bulldog with her teeth in my calf, and the charade has to be held up. Blowing our cover means alienating Consolidated Evalu-shop's other major client. Greg has held on to this long-standing contract for years, and while we all joke about how boring evaluations for banks, credit unions, lending companies, and insurance can be, it pays the bills and keeps the marketing company where I work afloat.

When a steady contract is at stake, I'm willing to leverage my (not so big) sense of dignity to keep the client happy.

Unfortunately, I took the same approach with Monica all those years, letting her digs and condescension chip away at me for the sake of Steve.

"You've gotten married?" she gasps, craning her neck around the credit union, looking for an obvious suspect. "Where is he?"

Amanda reaches for my hand and pulls me close, her shoulder banging against mine as she bends down and kisses my cheek. "He is she. Me. We're the newlyweds."

Monica's social mask doesn't just crack. It shatters. "You're, you're…" Her mouth twists like she's accidentally eaten a live gecko. "Lesbians?" The word emerges like that goopy, growling head from John Hurt's stomach in *Alien*.

Amanda looks at her watch and doesn't answer the question while I do my best imitation of a twelve-pound sea bass being pulled onto a ship with a hook in its eye and mouth opening and closing, unaware of its pending slow, painful death.

"We both have an appointment in thirty minutes, so could we move on?" Amanda says to Jim in a *don't you dare say no* voice. Powerful and commanding, she's also casual in an enviable way. I almost want to date her. Wait. I'm married to her. I can't date her.

Jim rallies. "Of course, of course! Monica, so good to see you," he says as he reaches to shake her hand. She snatches it away, and instead those demon eyes glare like twin rubies, pointed at me.

"You're a lesbian? A married lesbian?" Her tone is that of a preschool teacher explaining that there are seven continents to a group of three-year-olds, as if I don't know what I am saying and she's correcting me. She sounds unhinged.

"Yes," I say in an out-breath, the word floating off on the air like a fart. She flinches.

Then her entire face morphs. Jim goes back to his desk and mutters something about getting the paperwork in place. One claw-like hand reaches for my upper arm and pulls me a few feet away from him, and now her words come out in a hurried hiss.

Amanda follows us, still holding my hand and grinning like a Disney character. If Monica is Maleficent, then Amanda has somehow turned into Dopey in seconds.

"You like women."

"I love women!" I chirp.

Her frown deepens, eyes flickering left and right as if retrieving memories to process. My hand starts to sweat and Amanda lets go of it, wiping it on her skirt. She shoots me a pleading look, as if to say there's nothing we can do about this.

And you know those news reports about people who have cars suddenly plunge through plate glass windows into storefronts and houses?

I now consider them lucky. *Oh please God, send one now.*

But no. Instead, Monica says, tapping a manicured index finger on her peach-coated lips, "It all makes much more sense now."

"What is that supposed to mean?" Amanda and I say at the exact same time in the exact same *WTF?* tone.

Monica's face transforms as she thinks, the locked jaw softening as seconds pass. "Oh, dear. No wonder you and Steve didn't work out. You were looking for a Boston Wife and he was looking for a wife in Boston."

A Boston Wife. I've heard the term before. Antiquated phrase used to mean lesbianism long before it was socially acceptable to say *lesbian.*

"I dated Steve and loved Steve and he rejected me," I say, a red cloud of fury growing over my head, ready to unleash a torrent of poison on Monica.

Jim clears his throat. Did he overhear that?

"Can you blame my son?" Monica is clutching imaginary pearls so hard I think she's giving herself a tracheotomy. "He sensed it. He's intelligent, and he's a man. A red-blooded, masculine man with needs. You clearly couldn't give him what he needed, so he left." She sniffs the air. The gesture is so snobby it makes me bark with laughter. Dame Maggie Smith could take lessons on aristocratic pretension from Monica.

"We are talking about the same Steve, right?"

Amanda asks me. "The same guy who wore his socks during sex and who insisted on making you buy all the Japanese tentacle erotica on your book account so it was never traced back to him?"

"Some things are meant to be private," Monica whispers in a scathing voice.

"Monica, he buys old Japanese prints from the Meiji period and puts them on his bedroom walls. Haven't you ever taken a good look at what's going on in those paintings? The octopus hanging on to the woman's half-naked body isn't there to be cuddled," I add.

Eyes widening, Monica looks like she might pass out. I start to feel guilty. I could really grind the knife in right now, but I don't.

"Your red-blooded, masculine man has some really weird Hentai fantasies," Amanda says flatly.

"Wait," Monica says, eyes clouded with confusion. She pulls out her phone and taps into what looks like her text message screen, then reads something. "Steve told me you're dating Declan McCormick now." Low whistle. "Impressive." Her eyes flicker to Amanda. "You accept the fact that Shannon is…bisexual?" That word seems easier for her to say than *lesbian*, but it still manages to come out sounding like she's accidentally bitten into a piece of chocolate-covered poop.

I freeze. Amanda does, too. What can we say? How do I explain to my fake wife that I have a real billionaire boyfriend?

Amanda laughs. "That's just business."

Monica's eyebrow shoots to the sky. "You're

pretending to date Declan McCormick? Even Jessica Coffin made a comment about you two as a couple."

Amanda grimaces. I know she follows Jessica on Twitter. This is a mess. Certified, Grade A, failed-shop mess. If I admit I'm dating Declan, the entire mystery shop falls apart. If I don't, Monica will start up the rumor mill into a DEFCON 1 level, complete with whooping sirens and fainting blue bloods.

I'd rather have my hand stuck in a toilet while eating hazelnut-flavored horseradish.

Amanda is cutting her eyes over to Jim so sharply she looks like she works for Wüsthof, and she squeezes me with more affection than a three-year-old meeting her first creation from Build-A-Bear. "Right, honey? You're just dating Declan to make a solid business deal even better."

Monica is eyeing me like my mom eyes a seventy-five-percent-off sale at Gaiam. "That's right." Fake smile. "I'm working on being more aggressive in business."

"Steve would be proud," his mom mutters. "He tried so hard to help you develop that killer instinct."

I open my mouth to say something, and Amanda presses her finger against my lips in what looks like an affectionate gesture.

"So you're really, truly not dating Declan McCormick for his looks? His charm? His money?" Monica persists.

"For his company's money," I say, instantly

hating the words on my mouth. Trying not to blow my cover means I'm about to blow chunks. Amanda squeezes my hand and nestles closer. I feel green. I'm Kermit the Frog right now.

"Everyone's so much happier now, aren't we? Steve certainly is." Amanda's words make Monica back down. She reaches into her purse and fiddles with something on her phone, then looks up at the wall clock.

Tight smiles all around. We look like the "After" picture from a two-for-one coupon for plastic surgery.

"Your mother must be very happy to have one of her girls married off." She pauses. "Again, I mean. I know Carol's divorced."

Oh, no.

"It was a simple, civil ceremony," I shoot back. "Not an actual wedding." I squeeze Amanda. "We're holding a wedding and reception quite soon."

"Really? Where?"

"At Farmington," Amanda blurts out.

Amanda doesn't realize that Monica is on the board of directors for Farmington Country Club.

"You *can't*." Monica's voice becomes low and roaring.

Jim happens to wander over at this exact moment. "Can't what?" He's holding a stack of printouts. I see a mortgage disclosure statement thicker than a thirteenth-century French stone castle wall in his beefy hands.

"Can't have a wedding at Farmington Country

149

Club," Monica says in hushed tones.

His expression is bemused. "Why not?"

Monica blanches. "Because it's not done."

"Weddings are done all the time there." His eyes narrow and his jaw tightens. Go Jim! You're getting one hell of an evaluation. At least, after I go puke in a trash can and take four Xanax.

Monica stiffens. "Of course." Smile so tight she could slice cheese with it. "We'll see about that," which, when translated from Bitchspeak, is actually *Oh hell no they won't*.

Jim gives me a searching look, then grants Amanda one as well. "Shall we?" He holds up the stack of papers. "You newlyweds have a home and a life to start building." He gives Monica a cold look. "Right this instant."

She frowns and pretends to answer her phone, her exit remarkably anti-climatic.

"Sorry about that," Jim says as we settle in. I'm guessing another hour or so of paperwork and then we can leave. If only my credit score were higher than my bra size.

"No problem. It happens," Amanda says. Her tone is neutral but I know she's testing Jim. My body is about to supernova with anger and parts of me will turn into ribbons of flesh that stretch into the parking lot and strangle Monica, so I stay silent and just brood.

"The truth is all over Shannon's face," Jim points out.

"The truth?"

He looks pointedly toward where Monica just

exited, sighs, and pulls out the first paper from the stack, clicking a ballpoint pen. "Some people would rather hide behind a mask than be vulnerable and real." His eyes are open and respectful, but something darker passes through them.

And with that, Jim just got the highest score possible on this mystery shop.

And I lost everything important to me because I couldn't ditch my mask.

Chapter Fourteen

The first person to message me is my sister, who does it to my face.

"Oh MY GOD," Amy screams as she crashes through my doorway, nearly flattening the cheap hollow-core door. Her hair springs to life around her like Medusa snakes as her neck snaps up and down between freaking out at whatever's on her phone screen and making eye contact with me that reminds me of the women in *The Handmaid's Tale* when they are sent off to their assignments.

"What did Mom do now?" I ask. Note to self: get deadbolt for bedroom door. Especially if I plan to have overnight guests.

Which I do.

"It's not Mom. This time. For once." She paces, her hair like a lady in waiting. I run my hand through my own locks and find a rat's nest of straight, stringy hair. How does she manage to look like a cross between Merida and Christina Hendricks while I look like a drunk Cameron Diaz in *Bad Teacher* combined with Melissa McCarthy after that unfortunate diarrhea scene in *Bridesmaids*?

Genetics.

"Then who?" I reach for my phone to check messages from Declan. He was working late last night and then had a board of directors meeting for some big charity organization. We're meeting tonight at my place for drinks. As in, he'll drink me and I'll drink him and eventually we'll cave in to basic sustenance needs and order Thai takeout.

"Jessica!"

"Jessica…who?" I'm rubbing my eyes, trying to wake up. Before being so rudely interrupted I was in the middle of a dream where Declan and I were in a cabana on a beach on some tropical island, naked and tanned and drinking something fruity and delightful out of a half coconut…

"Coffin!"

"Jessica Coffin." I say the name slowly, then open my messaging app.

157 messages.

Say wha?

"Why do I have 157 messages? Steve isn't THAT crazy!" I shout.

Amy throws her hands in the air in exasperation. It just makes her look cuter. If I do it, I look like I'm swatting flies. "That's what I'm trying to tell you!" Her eyes are filled with panic and pity. "Your life blew up last night in cyberspace." She pauses. "And, soon, real life. Have you heard from Billionaire Boy?"

"What the hell does Declan have to do with anything?"

The front door opens and someone shouts "Hello—oh, Jesus! Leave me alone! Those are new

154

shoes!"

"Chuckles!" Amy and I shout at the same time. The cat had his balls hacked off forever ago but sometimes he still marks his territory, especially on shoes with laces that go up the ankle. As Amanda stumbles into my room shaking her foot, I see I'm right.

"Why are you wearing gladiator sandals in my place? You know Chuckles pees on them."

"Forgive me for forgetting that you have a cat with a lace fetish," she says back, fuming. "They're in style right now." She grabs a towel draped across the back of a chair and starts wiping her foot, cursing under her breath as she teeters off to the bathroom. The faucet turns on just as Amy zeroes in on me.

I cut her off. "Coffee? I can't handle a crisis before I've had three cups."

"Tough luck, sis, because the crisis is here whether you're caffeinated or not."

"And what, exactly, is the crisis?"

She points to my phone.

157 messages.

"Read those while I make you a double espresso. You're going to need it." Her ominous warning makes me frown, and Chuckles wanders in with a disapproving look that makes me scan the room for laces of any kind.

Fortunately, I have a taste in shoes that veers pretty close to that of a skateboarder, so I'm safe.

He sniffs the air, narrows his eyes, and looks at the phone in my hand. *Go ahead,* he seems to say.

Make my day.

Now my cat is giving me Dirty Harry lines. This is worse than I thought.

"But before you read your messages, you need to read Jessica Coffin's Twitter feed," Amanda explains as she comes out of the bathroom shoeless. "It's...well, honey," she says with a compassion that makes my heart race. "Honey, you need to have that coffee in you."

'Honey' is what Declan calls me, I almost cry out. It sounds pathetic and ominous when Amanda does it.

"How bad can some frozen woman's Twitter feed be? What does it have to do with my life?" They're scaring me. She's just some woman Steve dated. Some woman who wanted Declan.

"Remember yesterday at the credit union?"

"How could I forget?"

"How we ran into Steve's mom?"

"Get to the point." Amy brings me a coffee and I take a sip, burning my tongue. The coffee could peel paint, it's so strong, but that appears to be intentional.

Oh, boy.

"Monica must have said something to Steve who said something to Jessica." Amanda and Amy share a look that makes my blood run cold. Chuckles smiles. I should rent him out as an interrogator for the Russian mob.

Oh, this is bad. Really bad.

"And Jessica—what? Mentioned me on her Twitter feed?" I make a huffy laughing sound.

Ludicrous. What's a Tweet going to do to me? Hurt my Klout score? Ouch. You hurt my fake internet feelings.

They look at me with alarm. "Yes," they say in unison.

I glare at Amanda. "I knew that tentacle porn comment would bring us nothing but trouble."

I reach for my phone in slow motion, like something out of *The Matrix*, except instead of feeling like I'm part of some kickass save-the-world moment, I feel like an insect that is two seconds away from being crushed by the windshield of a Mini Cooper.

Amanda holds her phone out to me as Amy stares at her and whispers, "Tentacle porn? Do I even want to ask?"

@jesscoffN says: *Lesbians who date billionaires to make big business deals. Sounds like a reality TV show or a trashy romance novel*

"That's it?" I laugh. "No one cares."

"Look at the stream that follows," Amy says in a voice you'd use to tell someone they've walked around in front of the CEO of their corporation with their skirt shoved in the waistband of their pantyhose.

@bigdealmkr: *Let me guess. SJ? Unbelievable*

"SJ? Shannon Jacoby? What? People talking about me online using my initials? C'mon, guys, this is…" My voice disappears as I read the rest. Bigdealmkr is Steve. I remember the day he picked his username.

@jesscoffN: *@bigdealmkr I guess some*

people are so desperate they'll stoop to anything, even cheating on their wife to make a business deal

"What? What?" I scream with laughter. "This is fucking hilarious!"

"Keep reading," Amanda urges, nudging my elbow so I'll drink more coffee. I suck down half the now-cooler cup and my eyes scan the page as I scroll through.

About twenty people asking Jessica to "dish" or "spill." Obviously scheduled tweets from Jessica for places to eat or shop.

"This is nothing!" I insist. And while a creepy, cold electric feeling is growing in my gut, I stand by that. I mean it. This is just stupid online social media crap that doesn't affect me in real life. Right?

"Look at the one that Tweets Declan."

"Declan?" That cold electric feeling sparks like someone's flipped a breaker.

@jesscoffN @anterdec2 How's business?

"That's no big deal." But my voice is shaking. I'm quivering, the vibrations deep inside, like a flock of birds has been scared by a distant gunshot and needs to flee, flying straight up without a plan or a pattern. Just panicking and needing to move.

Thousands of birds inside me begin their sudden migration, but there's no way out. They bang into my bones, my skin, my muscles.

"He never responds," Amy says quickly, eyes wide and so blue I want to swim in them.

"Why would he? He knows it's bullshit." But that's the problem, I fear: does he? When you don't know what people are saying about you to others behind your back, all you're left with is your own crazy imagination. And I have a penchant for self-torture that is so strong I should headline at a masochists' convention.

"Check your messages. Maybe he texted or called."

My fingers feel like icicles as I fumble with my phone. No voice mail. A quick scan of my email shows a few communications with mystery shoppers who encountered problems, a couple who lost receipts, and a ton of junk mail.

157 text messages.

I open the app with a finger that feels like I'm pushing the nuclear war button.

I'm getting tweets from people in high school who didn't bother to acknowledge I existed back then. People who openly mocked me. And is that my former orthodontist? Christ. Who's next? My gynecolo—

Yep. @openwide123—that's the gynecologist, not the ortho.

Most of the messages, though, are gibberish from people I don't know, all from Twitter. I opened an account a few years ago but barely use it. Did someone loop me into the @jesscoffN conversation?

Amy explains. "Steve did it. He referenced you. You can see it in his feed."

"We can explain this to Declan," Amanda whispers as I groan.

I ignore her, searching my messages. Nothing from Declan. Nothing. Not a word. Silence is worse than outrage.

Much worse.

"We have a meeting today with him," Amanda adds.

"Who?" My voice sounds like it's coming from the end of a very long tunnel.

"Declan. We're meeting with Anterdec today."

Chapter Fifteen

"Oh, God." I pull the covers over my head like it will accomplish something. Inside my white, billowy pretend cloud of escape, I wish I could go back to being five years old, when the worst thing that could happen to me was to have to wear the wrong colored ribbon.

Amy comes back in. "Shannon? Come out from under there," she insists. I pop my head out like a turtle checking it out after an atom bomb's been dropped.

In my panic I hadn't noticed she took my empty coffee cup and now she's returning with a full one. When did she become so servile? Ever since I met Declan she's been waiting on me. Not that I mind—coffee in bed is best served by a naked man who smells like sex, but a close second is, well...*anyone* delivering hot coffee in bed.

I reach for the cup, grateful. "Thanks."

"No text from Declan?" she asks, pointing to my phone.

"Nope."

"You're sure? With a bazillion messages you might have missed one."

"Go ahead." I point my chin at my own

smartphone. "See for yourself. Or," I add, taking a long sip of coffee, "*don't* see. There's nothing to see. He's dumped me, hasn't he?"

A big, tight wave of pain and lust billows through me. It's the feeling of tidal waves pulling back from shore, exposing all the starfish and hermit crabs to the sun and air, helpless and at the mercy of a force of nature so much stronger.

Jessica Twitterhead Coffin.

"That Tweet wasn't so bad."

"It's pretty incriminating," I mumble. I can't believe my life has imploded because of comments made in 140 characters or less. If brevity is the soul of wit, then Twitter is the steaming pile of manure at the end of the horse. Yeah, I know that comparison made no sense, but I'm sitting here in bed with 157 text messages, most of them from people with Twitter handles like @lebronsux4ever and @mygunmyheart and I'm supposed to have a cogent reaction?

And not one damn message from Declan or @anterdec2 or...

"Wait." I snap my neck up at Amanda, who, I realize, is now a redhead. Her hair is the exact same color as Amy's. I narrow my eyes. "You said we have a meeting with Declan today?"

"And James and...Andrew." I can see long strands of drool coming out of her bright-red-painted mouth when she says that last word. Great. Now my best friend wants to hump my boyfriend's brother. This could be a sitcom.

Except a good sitcom needs a crazy mother to

invade at just the right moment. I pause, because if ever there were a time for Mom to appear, it would be now. I close my eyes, cross my legs, and just... wait.

Chuckles climbs on my bed and settles into my lap. This must be worse than I thought if he's offering me comfort. You know how those nature shows on cable TV talk about how animals have a preternatural instinct to sniff out natural disasters like tornadoes and earthquakes before they happen?

Uh oh.

"Why did you just go blank?" Amy asks. She keeps wandering in and out of the room and I see why. Her hair is pulled up now in a perfect up-do, one long, springy curl cascading down around each ear. Her work suit is cut to fit her curves and she's inserting a simple pearl earring into one creamy lobe.

"Why do you look like a young Chelsea Clinton?"

She beams. "Do I? Because she worked for venture capital firms, too, and now she makes $600,000 a year!" My inadvertent compliment makes me forget, for a split second, the mess in cyberspace I apparently need to deal with in real life. At Anterdec.

Today.

"I think that $600,000 has something to do with her last name, Amy."

"Whatever." Amy fluffs her hair. "If I can make half that I don't need to chase billionaires."

Ouch. Chuckles leaps off my lap and gives her

ankles a rub. Too bad she's not wearing laces. His head twitches around and our eyes lock, as if my damn cat read my mind.

"What time is the meeting?" I ask Amanda.

"One o'clock. But Greg wants to have a strategy session before we go."

"Strategy session?"

"James McCormick wants us to start evaluating his high-end properties immediately. They've experienced a significant financial loss over the past two quarters at their major hotels, specifically." She claps her hands with joy, like Pee Wee Herman. "We're gonna shop The Fort! We're gonna shop The Fort."

All I can manage is a scowl. "One o'clock." Can I wait that long?

My damn mind-reading friend says, "Text him. Call him."

"He didn't text or call me!"

"Maybe he's just busy."

"Amanda, he was sexting nonstop after our last date, and then he goes cold." I hold up a finger to get her to pause. She's sliding her shoes back on, and I want to warn her, but...

I type *Please call me* and click send, hoping he replies.

She watches me, and when I'm done Amanda says, "Maybe he lost his phone in a toilet?"

I throw a pillow at her. Chuckles chases after it, then stops at her foot. I open my mouth to say something but it's too late.

"Jesus Christ!" she screams as a thin stream of

yellow pee hits her foot. She limps back into the bathroom, whimpering something that sounds close to a Scottish curse you'd hear Geillis Duncan mutter in one of the *Outlander* books.

Chuckles looks back and me and I swear he winks.

"Bad kitty," I mutter through a smile.

"Did you train him to do that? Why does he pee on laces and gladiator shoes, of all things?"

"Your kink is not my kink," Amy says as she slings her leather bag over her shoulder. She really does look like a commanding businesswoman, ready to take on a boardroom full of investors, cat-pee-free and blissfully unencumbered by Twitter rumors about her sociopathic use of a bad-boy billionaire to clinch a business deal while cheating on her lesbian wife.

Say that five times fast.

"What does that even mean?" Amanda shouts from the other room. "I don't have a kink. I'm vanilla."

"Nobody's truly vanilla," Amy scoffs. She gives me a mischievous look, playing Amanda. "You have to have a kink. Getting golden showers from Grumpy Cat, for instance."

"Golden *what*?"

Amy frowns at me. "And *she's* the one who gets to do sexy toy store evaluations?" She shakes her head sadly but, thankfully, does not elaborate.

"No, but Mom offered to go with her on those."

Amy's face twists with agony. "Poor Amanda."

"Right. Mom has a kink or two she can lend."

"I don't need a kink!" Amanda insists, walking into my bedroom smelling like the orange air freshener spray we keep in there.

"Everyone needs a kink," Amy and I say in unison.

And it was like saying *Beetlejuice, Beetlejuice, Beetlejuice*, because my front door opens and in walks my mom.

"You summoned her!" Amanda hisses. She's holding her sandals again, and turns to my closet just as Mom walks into the scene. "You better have some nice shoes I can borrow."

Mom looks at Amanda's shoes and immediately whips around to look at Chuckles, who is staring into the mirror on the back of my bedroom door and hissing at that strange cat.

"You wore shoes with long laces around *him*?" Mom giggles and shakes her head slowly. "I'm so sorry."

"Why are *you* sorry?" I ask.

"That's my fault. Um..." Her brow furrows. "Actually, it's your father's fault. He wore that gladiator outfit that one time we got into this little role play where I pretended to be tied up for the Kraken to come and take me, and Chuckles panicked. He peed all over Jason's feet and I haven't been able to wear a pair of sandals with ankle laces ever since."

Amy freezes in the doorway.

"But Marie, the Kraken...why would you use that in a bedroom role play?" Amanda's muted voice calls back. She's buried in my closet. I see her ass poking out and I want to kick it.

"Don't provoke her! I don't want to hear!" Amy dashes out the door. I hear the apartment door slam. My fingers are in my ears as I say "tra-la-la-la-la" as loudly as I can to drown out whatever depravity-laden story Mom is oversharing.

Amanda's distinctly paling face tells me I need to keep up my verbal assault. Even Chuckles looks a shade or two lighter than usual.

"Shannon! Shannon! You can pull your fingers out of your ears," she says with exasperation, as if I am the transgressor.

Amanda mouths *Be careful*.

I pull my fingers out and Mom says, "You're coming to my yoga class on Friday." It's Tuesday, so I have three days to agree and then come up with a really lame excuse to back out. Agnes might rough me up in the alley if I show my face without Declan's ass.

"Okay," I say.

"And no excuses! Chuckles did not have a leg amputated, like you said last month to get out of coming."

Damn. Chuckles examines his front paw with a distinct expression of relief. Great. I'm going to come home to find he's used my jelly bean stash as a litter box, aren't I?

"Sorry, bud," I whisper to him from across the room. "I'll bring home some catnip. Please don't eat the computer cords again."

Amanda and I share one of those looks where a

series of weird, covert gestures and eyebrow movements somehow translates into facial semaphore code. *Does Mom know about me and Declan and the Twitter mess?* is my basic question.

Seventy-two twitches and grimaces later, the answer is *no*.

Whew.

"Marie, we're very late for work," Amanda says. "How about I make us a coffee while Shannon showers?"

Mom's eyes narrow to black-smudged triangles. Whenever any of her daughters are too nice to her, she's suspicious, and Amanda's her fourth kid in her mind.

"Is Declan in the bedroom?" she says with glee. "Is that why you're acting so weird?"

I wish.

"If he were?" Amanda says. Ouch. Shoot me through the heart, but I see her point. Mom starts to back out slowly. It's not technically a lie, right?

Then she stops and looks at Amanda, hard. "If he's here, why are *you* in the bedroom?"

Amanda slowly, exquisitely, arches one eyebrow and stares Mom down. It's like Laura Prepon in *That '70s Show* and *Orange is the New Black* with a heaping dose of Angelina Jolie thrown in.

Mom's look of horror is beyond perfect. "I, um, uh, I have to go," she says quickly. We hear the apartment door slam and Chuckles gives Amanda an admiring look and lifts his front paw toward her like a high-five.

168

"I can't believe you implied we're having a threesome," I squeak out. But hot damn, it worked! I need to file that little strategy away next time Mom comes over and wants me to get a Brazilian or those pedicures where the fish eat all the dead skin.

"I can't believe some role play kink between her and your dad makes your cat piss all over my shoes."

"Touché."

Tears threaten to push through and I can't quite catch my breath. What if it's over before we really got started? So much is there with Declan, and I—

Amanda's steady hand presses into my shoulder. "If it's any consolation, the early reports are coming in from the credit unions and there is clear discrimination going on in at least two branches. The LGBT mortgage program will help weed that out. You might want a divorce, but—"

I stick my tongue out at her.

"—but we made a difference."

That makes me cry, finally. "Great. Can't even wallow in self-pity," I sniff. "I may have screwed up my one chance at happiness with a great guy, but we also made a difference and helped people."

"Don't look so glum."

I sigh. "I know. It's just…I don't regret doing the shop, but at the same time, let me feel what I feel. Okay? I can feel two conflicting emotions at the same time. It's called being human."

A few beats of silence stretch between us. And a handful of sniffles.

"Get your butt in the shower and let's go see

Declan and figure this all out. The longer you cower in the bed, the stupider this gets. Don't let a Tweet dictate your life," she counsels.

"When did you become a philosopher?" I stalk off to the bathroom without waiting to hear her answer.

"When your cat turned my foot into a litter box." She taps Chuckles' extended paw and I swear he separates his little toes and gives a "peace out" sign.

"What if he...what if I...oh, God." My hands shake and my heart feels like it wants to run away and bury its head in a giant vat of double-chocolate brownie ice cream.

Amanda's sympathetic face comes into view through the hair curtain I have covering me. "The only way to know what Declan is thinking or feeling is to go see him."

"What if I've blown it?"

"You don't know that you did."

"Easter was so special."

"Then you have nothing to worry about," she declares. "No guy shows up for a holiday with the family and then ditches a woman because of a stupid tweet."

"Really?"

She shrugs. "I don't know. That sounded like a supportive thing to say."

"Too much honesty is not a good thing."

"No kidding." She sighs. "Why do you think I'm still single?"

I blink back my tears. "But not enough honesty

170

gets you tweets from a woman who looks like something out of Madame Tussaud's wax museum."

My phone buzzes.

We both freeze.

It's Declan.

* * *

Continued in *Shopping for a Billionaire 4*, the end of the Shopping for a Billionaire series…

Sign up for my New Releases and Sales email list at my blog to get an email as soon as the final part of the Shopping series is published!

http://jkentauthor.blogspot.com/p/sign-up-for-my-new-releases-email-list.html

Other Books by Julia Kent

Suggested Reading Order

Her First Billionaire—FREE
Her Second Billionaires
Her Two Billionaires
Her Two Billionaires and a Baby
Her Billionaires: Boxed Set

It's Complicated

Complete Abandon (A Her Billionaires novella)
Complete Harmony (A Her Billionaires novella #2)

Random Acts of Crazy
Random Acts of Trust
Random Acts of Fantasy
Random Acts of Hope

"Share Me" in the anthology Spring Fling

Maliciously Obedient
Suspiciously Obedient

Deliciously Obedient (the trilogy is done!)

Shopping for a Billionaire 1
Shopping for a Billionaire 2

About the Author

Text JKentBooks to 77948 and get a text message on release dates!

New York Times and *USA Today* bestselling author Julia Kent turned to writing contemporary romance after deciding that life is too short not to have fun. She writes romantic comedy with an edge, and new adult books that push contemporary boundaries. From billionaires to BBWs to rock stars, Julia finds a sensual, goofy joy in every book she writes, but unlike Trevor from *Random Acts of Crazy*, she has never kissed a chicken.

She loves to hear from her readers by email at jkentauthor@gmail.com,

on Twitter @jkentauthor, and on Facebook at https://www.facebook.com/jkentauthor

Visit her blog at http://jkentauthor.blogspot.com

Made in the USA
San Bernardino, CA
28 November 2014